Adventures of a
Sex Addict

Sherry Marie Somerville

ISBN 978-0-9951914-6-4

Table of Contents

Foreplay

My name is Sherry Somerville. I was a morose child a withdrawn teenager and a resigned young woman. My secretarial job at Industrial Life was uneventful and at twenty-five, I married the company accountant. For six years, every Saturday night, Harold, my husband, would lay on top of me, move up and down faster and faster until he groaned, or grunted—or both—and rolled off.

For the first month, I'd squeal and bounce with him, imitating the X-rated movies he watched every Saturday night before he climbed on top of me, but after that, I would just lie there and wait till he finished. On our sixth anniversary, he got hit by a car and died instantly. I think it was the most exciting thing that ever happened to him.

In my thirties, I searched for my purpose in life. I tried yoga, power walking, kick boxing and step dancing. In my forties, I tried quilting, water colour painting and scrap booking, but nothing grabbed my interest.

For my 50th birthday, my friends and colleagues at Industrial Life threw a surprise party for me. It wasn't the only surprise I got that night. After the shouts and laughter and drinks and cake and presents, I got the biggest surprise of my life. It happened like this.

1: Awakening

It had been a grand birthday party. The beginning of a new decade. What new activity would I try now to give me some purpose in life? Maybe reincarnation? Or the Tarot?

At the end of the evening, I gathered my gifts, and as I was saying my thank you's and good bye's, Tom Richards from Advertising offered to drive me home. Tom was an Aussie who had only been with the company for three weeks. Jeannette, at personnel, had passed the lowdown on him to all the girls in the office. He was twenty seven, single and drove a vintage Austin Healy. We didn't need to be told he was drop-dead good looking, six feet tall and regularly worked out at the gym.

The other women raised their eyebrows and tittered when I walked out with Mr. Awesome. Little did I realize that the next hour would change my life. That I would be propelled into places and feelings I never dreamed existed. That I would not only find my purpose but a whole new reason and passion for living.

But right now I simple enjoyed having a handsome young man carry my parcels, help me in and out of his low slung vehicle and walk me to the entrance of the Victoria Gardens Complex where I lived.

"Let me help you to your apartment," he said, his arms full of birthday packages.

"Thank you, Tom. That's very kind of you." Such a nice young man.

We didn't speak in the elevator or as we walked along the eleventh-floor hallway. I fumbled for my key, opened the door and we entered.

I pointed to the beige paisley couch. "Just put them there."

He tumbled the parcels out of his arms, turned to me and said, "Happy Birthday. See you Monday." He leaned over and brushed a light kiss on my cheek. I must have moved slightly because his lips touched the corner of my mouth. A spark jumped between us.

"Oh my," I said. A tingle skipped through my solar plexus.

"Oh, wow," he said. He put his full lips on mine and stayed there. I didn't move away.

His tongue pushed my mouth open. My body pressed against him while my tongue met his equally probing snake.

Harold had never kissed me like this. No one had ever kissed me like this. What was happening to me? My body was on fire. I wanted—no needed—this young man to engulf me and I him.

We tore at our clothing and each others: yanking at buttons, pulling zippers, feverish to touch, to feel, to have.

Reason completely left me. I was a wild animal swamped with desire.

With one swift movement, he ripped my underpants apart and his throbbing hardness found my wet entrance. We fell onto my birthday gifts, shoving them aside, and there amongst ribbons and wrappings, in less than a moment I, Sherry Marie Somerville, experienced the big O for the first time in my life. O with a capital letter. O as in OMG! O as in OOOOHHHH!!!

Yes, I had my first orgasm. My body quivered and shivered and shook. The earth stood still and the heavens exploded in a canopy of fireworks while the 1812 Overture resounded in my head.

I had found my purpose. This was what life was all about. After that incredible burst of quantum energy, I collapsed and lay replete and at peace, floating in a bubble of wholeness and plenitude. Filled up. Satiated. Connected to every particle in the Universe. At one with God.

The man named Tom pulled out of me. "What just happened?"

"Life just happened," I murmured as I swooned in delicious ecstasy.

The next morning I woke up in bed naked. I put both hands t my head as I slowly regained consciousness. *I must have had a little too much to drink.* I was never a hard drinker and hadn't had a hangover since I'd turned twenty-one when I decided on that birthday to be an adult. *And how come I'm naked? I never sleep naked.* What would the nuns think of such shameless behaviour?

My mouth was dry and tasted like stale gin. I threw off the covers, pulled on my housecoat and padded to the bathroom for a drink of water. Two glasses and a quick pee later I grabbed my housecoat and walked into the living room. Presents and loose wrappings lay scattered on my couch and floor.

"What the hell?" A surge of energy shot up my body. "Holy Baloney! Tom!" The memory of last night surged through me and that seminal moment when that dear sweet throbbing man had swept me into other realms.

My untied housecoat hung loose, my naked body brazenly exposed. But the most alarming thing was, I didn't give a hoot.

"So what?" The nuns can't whip me now. The priest can't make me deny my womanhood and I had long ago let go of the fear of Hell and damnation. Up until last night, sex had been so ho hum in my life, I couldn't imagine God really thinking it was a sin.

But now! How I could I have missed it all these years? Sure, I learned about sex in school like everybody else, but the fear of God and burning in Hell for eternity had kept me far away from any male person.

But when I was fourteen in my sixth foster home, that nice Catholic boy climbed into my bed. I was still half asleep when I woke up to find him fiddling between my legs. Sure, I was scared but curious and when he finished, I remember thinking. What's the big deal? Why is this such a big sin? And how come it was okay to do it once you were married and even then only to have babies. Well, I sure didn't want any babies, so that was a good reason not to do it. But older boys had this rubbery thing they would put on and one of my foster sisters told me about pills to take. God had not struck me dead for letting boys stick their thing in me and they enjoyed it so much, I thought what the hell, it's better than being alone.

Some girls I knew enjoyed it and I pretended to as well. Boys and men liked it when you panted and squealed and said things, like, "Oh, yes, yes. That's it. Do it again. Do it harder. More, more." I became a really good actress and got some pleasure out of bringing men so much.

I thought when I got married, that God and Harold would bring me what I was missing. I looked so forward to my wedding night but it was same ol', same ol'. He grunted and hollered and I panted and said, "Yes, Yes" and then it was over. Five years into my marriage, I tried it with another man but nothing, so I gave up.

That is until last night. On my glorious birthday, when dear Tom, bless him, spread my legs and opened my gates to heavenly bliss.

Here I was fifty (the new thirty thank goodness) and looking forward to some good years of exploring this new person I had become.

2: Getting My Feet Wet

All weekend, I could hardly wait until Monday to see Tom again. I didn't have his home number and he didn't call. Why would he? I was old enough to be his mother. Was he thinking that too? On Monday, Tom was out on call all day with new clients. On Tuesday I caught a glimpse of him in the cafeteria. I had no reason to go to Advertising, except to find out if last Friday had been an anomaly.

What secret spot had he aroused in me? Had he found the sacred G spot I had read about. I never dreamt there was so much pleasure hiding between my legs.

Tuesday night, alone in bed, I pulled my nighty up and felt around. My fingers touched a little knob. That felt good so I gently squeezed and rubbed it. It tingled and sent a thrill down my thighs. More rubbing led to more and more. I moved my hips up and down, my fingers slipping and sliding around the moist bed of pleasure.

"Oh, yes. That's it," I cried and rubbed harder and deeper until I arched in ecstasy as fire rockets went off: between my legs, in my head, through my stomach, down my legs. Breathing hard, with my body pulsating against my fingers inside me, I lay spinning through time and space. Finally, I pulled my hand away. It felt like hot sword being unsheathed. I gasped. I wanted that again. I wanted Tom's Excaliber inside me.

On Wednesday, he texted. Did I want to have a drink after work? Yes, I texted back. At 5:05 I climbed into his Austin Healy and he thundered off. We didn't go to the bar where the office employees routinely went on Friday.

He went eight blocks further and pulled up to an English pub. He ordered Guinness for us both. I had never tasted it before but I liked its strong and hearty flavour. Neither of us spoke about the birthday gift he'd given me last Friday night. We'd had quite a bit of wine at my party. Maybe he'd forgotten. Maybe it was nothing new for him. But why did he ask me out now?

"How are things in Advertising?" I said. *What a lame question.*

"Great. I'm working on a new campaign."

"That sounds good." I took a swig of beer.

"Say. Would you give me your opinion of it? It's on my laptop at home. Do you mind?"

My thighs tingled. "Not at all. I'd be glad to."

His apartment was what one would expect of a successful executive and bachelor. Modern furniture, a gigantic smart TV, Alexis following is commands and a butter soft brown leather couch. He stood behind me and reached up to remove my jacket. His touch tingled down my body.

His hand on me was like a switch ready to detonate an explosion. He spun me around and our mouths locked in a frantic kiss, tongues thrusting as our hands grabbed at each other. He peeled off my jacket, quickly followed by my blouse and bra. I stood half naked and his mouth moved to my nipples, kissing and licking. I unbuttoned my skirt and let it fall to the floor. He—or was it I—pushed my panty hose, along with my pants, down. I stepped out of them and he opened his fly, letting free an erect penis.

He grabbed it in one hand and pushed it inside me. Then he grasped my bottom and slammed it against his ramming sword. I threw my head back and surrendered to his pounding and to the boiling stream bubbling inside me. Up and up I went—a wild horse bucking at me. I thought it was the end of me. I will die pierced on his sword, his burning staff charging in and out of me with a flurry of madness. At the top of Everest, we exploded. Hot juice filled my inner spaces, spiralling me into orbit. My knees turned to jelly and he picked me up and carried me to the bedroom.

He laid me on the king sized bed. I was too satiated to feel anything but bliss. I half opened my eyes, and watched him take off his tie, his shirt, his pants and his underpants. What a beautiful body. Firm and strong.

In his full nakedness, he knelt beside the bed, leaned over and licked my breasts. He nibbled on my nipples, making them rise again. Then he kissed my bush and stuck his tongue into my clit. (I learned that word from the internet.) He nibbled, licked and sucked my magic spot, making me wriggle and bounce against his mouth and then he climbed on me, laying his body over me and pushed his hard probing wonderful delicious cock into me.

And so began my descent or ascent (depending on your philosophy) into the realm of radiant—to die for—or to live for, unbridled wanton sex.

3: Office Sex

Next day, at work, the girls asked me what I had been doing.

"What do you mean?" I said with an innocent look. I thought my rendezvous with Tom was well hidden.

"You look great. Ten years younger," said Helen.

"And there's a bounce to your step. One would think you've found a man," said Irene.

"It must be that new breakfast cereal," I said and hustled back to my desk for a day's work. One must be careful. Office gossip can start on a dime and roll into a thousand.

It was difficult working each day, seeing Tom and not touching him or having him touch me. It wasn't long before we were getting together one or two evenings a week, but it wasn't enough for me. I started to notice the bulge in men's pants. I never realized how horny men were. Sure, I'd heard of it. Other girls talked of it, but I just never noticed it before. Now it seemed my eyes went to their crotch first. I bought two new blouses with low cut necklines. I liked it when men talked to me with their eyes staring at my cleavage while I watched the front of their pants bulge out.

After one evening of particularly rousing sex, Tom told me he was going away for a week.

"Oh, no. What will I do without Peter?" (That's what he called his favourite body part.) "I'll miss him." And I kissed his favourite body part back to life again. Peter was always happy to be plunging into my new favourite body part again and again.

* * *

Work on Monday without Tom around was boring. I fidgeted all day, knowing I wasn't going to see him (or Peter) for a whole week. Yes, I could masturbate and I was doing that more often, but it wasn't the same. I wanted a full and throbbing penis inside me to carry me up the mountainside and off to the moon.

On Tuesday, I went into Tom's office and sat on his chair and stuck my hand between my legs. Slowly I stroked the silk strip covering my gateway to joy. It was starting to feel good, so I got up and locked the door, went back to his desk and took off my underpants. I lifted my skirt and wriggle my bare bum into his chair. Just when I was reaching my hand down again to touch my pleasure place, a knock sounded.

"Ms. Somerville. Can I see you for a moment?"

I sighed, stuck my pants in the drawer, and went to the door. "Sorry I didn't realize it was locked." It was Arnold from accounting.

"I need some figures from Tom's files. What are you doing in here?"

"Oh, I needed something from Tom too." I locked the door again.

"Why are you doing that?"

"I don't like to be disturbed when I am searching for something."

"Oh." He walked to the four-drawer filing cabinet and opened the top one.

"Are you married, Arnold?"

"No."

"What do you do for sex?"

He dropped the paper he had just taken out and I bent down and picked it up. On my upward ascent, I flicked open the top button of my already low cut blouse. Just as I reached his face, two mounds of bare and ample flesh pushed their way over my new lacy bra.

"I—I—"

"Oh, don't be embarrassed, Arnold. I'm taking a psychology course and we have to do a survey on the sexual practices of unmarried men."

"Oh."

"Sex is a normal part of life. So what do you do to satisfy yourself?"

His face turned red and he fumbled with the file in his hand. "I—I masturbate."

"Oh, that's nice. How often."

"Every morning. In—in the shower."

"Do you ever do it with women?" I stepped closer to him.

He pulled his head in like a turtle. "Not—not for a long time. I used to have a girlfriend but she didn't like it much."

"That's too bad." I took the file from his hand, tucked it into the drawer and shut it. I glanced down. The bulge was there. A large one. I put my hand on it and he jumped. "Relax, Arnold. It's only a psychology survey."

I took his hand and slid it up my thigh and over a bare hip. He gasped.

"Let's see what we have here," I said, as I unzipped his fly. I reached into his shorts and pulled out a huge erect penis. "Oh, my this is a dandy. What do you call it?" Droplets of moisture ran down my inner leg.

"Soldier," he croaked.

"Well, he certainly is standing to attention now." I lifted my skirt. "Let's put him to work." I wriggled on top of it.

He grabbed my bare bum and thrust his hips forward, pulling me to him, grunting and groaning like a strangled animal.

I rode soldier like a roller coaster. Up and down and up and down until I started the climb to the magical mountain. Up, up, up. My body alive with sparkles and diamonds and spikes of pleasure, too exquisite for words. He came with a thunder and I squeezed the soldier and burst with him. My knees gave way and he held me up with his hands clutching my bottom. We stayed joined while we regained normal breathing.

When he did withdraw, I gasped from the loss. "We must do this again."

"Oh, yes, I would like that." His breathing was still a little irregular. "Tomorrow? Here? Same time."

I smiled. "Why not?"

He tucked soldier away and zipped up. He ran to the door, slid the bolt open and darted out. He had forgotten his file.

The next day, at the exact same time, he came in, already bulging.

I was prepared. No underpants. He didn't make it to the filing cabinet. I walked up to him and lifted my skirt. He had his zipper open in a flash. Soldier was aimed and ready for duty. Just as he plunged it in, the door opened. We froze.

A male voice said, "Oh, sorry. I didn't know anyone was in here."

"Arnold was just helping me get something out of my eye," I said.

"Can I help?"

"No," I said. "It's still in, but I think he can manage it. He'll have it out in a moment."

As the visitor waited by the door, Soldier slipped out and Arnold fumbled with his zipper.

I stepped back saying, "There. It's out now. All is well."

Arnold went to the file cabinet, and the intruder went to Tom's desk, took a flash drive from the drawer and exited.

Even though the door was not locked, Arnold unzipped, and pulled out soldier again who soon found his way home. My heart beat faster, thinking someone might come in and find us bouncing against each other.

4: The Intruder Comes

That night, I thought about how well it had gone with Arnold. How easy and fun to have him do it to me. I thought Tom had the magic touch, but maybe it was all men. Hmmmm.

For most of Wednesday, I couldn't get away from my desk to visit Tom's office. Arnold passed by my desk four times with a lift of an eyebrow and a tilt of the head toward Tom's office, but what could I do?

Finally at 4:30 I made an excuse that I needed something from Tom's office and hurried down the hall, around the corner and inside. Would Arnold try the door? Had he given up? It was much later than our previous meeting.

The door opened and I eagerly looked up. It wasn't Arnold. It was the intruder from yesterday.

He closed the door behind him, and slid the bolt shut. "How's your eye? Did Arnold fix you up?"

"Er—well, yes he did."

He walked toward the desk where I was sitting and put out his hand. "I'm Jasper Stevens."

I stood up and took his hand. I knew his name but had never met the CEO of the company. "How do you do, sir."

"Please call me Jasper." He held my hand and put his other one on top of both of both of ours. "And you are?"

"Sherry Somerville." My voice shook. This was the big boss. "Accounting." *Is he going to fire me?* Then I noticed the bulge.

He smiled and stared at my plunging neckline.

"Can I get you something?" I asked.

"Yes. I think you can. Perhaps something like Arnold got yesterday." He smiled. "After he took that thing out of your —eye."

A rush of heat swam up my thighs and set fire to my lower half. "Am I fired?"

"Fired? No. not from your office job. But I hope you're fired up for this." He let go of my hand and put both of his on my breasts. "If that's all right with you."

I looked up at him, my clitoris nub tingling. "Yes, sir. I mean Jasper. That's more than all right."

We stared at each other as his hands got busy. First he slowly undid my blouse all the way. Then he reached around and unsnapped my bra. My full breasts were free and waiting for his touch..

He pushed his face into them. Rubbing and licking and sucking. "Oh, mamma," he mumbled. "Come to poppa."

I was getting hotter and hotter. I would have to masturbate big time if he didn't do something soon.

He did. He pulled my skirt up and reached under, gasping when he found no pants to wrangle with. He grabbed each side and pulled it all the way up to my waist. (I wore a full one on purpose).

Then he picked me up, sat me on the edge of the desk and buried his face between my legs. I lay back in heave while he licked and sucked and nibbled on my thrumming twat. (I also learned that word from the internet.)

I stuck my fist in my mouth to stop my screams of delight. I didn't want the whole office staff barging in right then. I pushed and wriggled against him and just when I couldn't stand it anymore, he lifted his dripping face, and pulled me up to sitting and instantly, his gigantic and stiff rod plunged into my begging opening.

He pushed his face into my boobs, pumping back and forth with slippery ease. "Momma, momma," he kept murmuring. "Come to poppa."

I held his head to my chest guiding his wet mouth from nipple to nipple. I was on a rocket ship to paradise, ready to explode. And explode we did. We both came with a whollop. I nearly fell off the desk, but he grabbed the edge holding us both up. We caught our breath and he pulled a huge handkerchief from his back pocket.

He wiped himself and my thighs off. "That was most satisfying, Miss Somerville."

"Call me Sherry," I said as I rearranged my bra and found the first button on my blouse.

Jasper zipped himself up and helped me off the desk. "My wife and I have sex on Saturday nights. On Thursday nights I visit a lady on the third floor of my apartment building."

I finished buttoning my blouse and smoothed my skirt down. *Why is he telling me about his sex life?*

He took my hand and said. "I will arrange for Tom to be on course for another week."

'Oh." What else could I say to the big boss? I had just learned how big he was.

"Do you and Tom fuck?"

The nuns said to never say that word but once I did and I got a licking on my bare behind by my foster father. It didn't hurt that much and now that I remember, I kinda liked lying over his lap, feeling a tingle between my legs. I had forgotten that.

"Well, do you?

"Well, yes we do."

"And do you fuck Arnold?"

He does like that word and I guess I am getting to be quite the fucker. "Yes, I do."

"I guess you like variety."

"I'm beginning to."

"I like fucking you. Do you like to fuck me?"

I had to be honest. "Yes, I do."

"Say it. Say you like to fuck me and you want me to fuck you again."

I hesitated, remembering the licking—and the tingling. My body still thrummed. "Yes sir. I like to fuck." I smiled. "And I want you, Jasper, to fuck me again."

He grinned, nodded, and walked out.

5: Getting Wetter

For the rest of that week, and all next, I enjoyed a daily duo of fucks. I had arranged with Arnold to meet him at 10:30 in Tom's office, and Jasper Stevens at 4:00. It was indeed a rousing week and when I awoke Saturday morning, I was glad I had a fuckless day ahead of me. It would give me time to rest my well used body part and a chance to consider where my life was going. With Tom returning, it was going to get complicated having sex with three men. I had a long leisurely bath before breakfast and had a long talk with my vagina.

"Well, partner. How are you doing? Getting stronger? It wasn't so long ago I was a virgin when it came to orgasm but you have to admit, I'm a quick and willing learner."

It's amazing that a body could want it so much. At least my body did. "How do you like those throbbing men parts inside us? Kinda cool, isn't it?" I reached into the water and lightly touched myself between my legs. Such a precious place. "I'm going to call you Virginia. Ginny for short." (I found out later that Ginny was also a name for my special lady parts.) I smiled at myself, thinking I had invented it.

It was fun to tease Virginia. She kept wanting more and something bigger inside her than my fingers. "You'll have to wait till Monday for the full Monty. Hmmm. Maybe I should buy a dildo. I could get one online and no one would know." Ginny fluttered in delight just thinking about it.

Sunday, I washed my hair and chose clothes to wear to work the next day. I didn't need to wear sexy clothes anymore. Men got into them fast enough anyway.

Monday was awkward. Tom was in his office and Arnold was all in a flap about where we could meet. By 10:30 we hadn't figured anything out so we had to skip our liaison. He walked around like a wounded puppy.

It was easy for Jasper. He had a private office and had me assigned to a special project. At 4:00 when I walked in, it was obvious what the project was. He was practically bursting out of his pants. He liked to do it with me sitting on the edge of the desk with my blouse open, but not off, bra and tits dangling. He never tired of the momma, poppa game of rubbing his face into my breasts as he drove his large cock into Virginia.

Ginny and I liked this game. I didn't care what turned him on, just as long as he kept fucking.

Near quitting time, Tom texted me. Did I want to go for a drink after work? Ginny was still throbbing from Jasper's visit but it was only fair that Tom get his share. After all he had been gone for two weeks and, bless his heart, he had started it all. I owed him.

We went to our usual bar eight blocks away and settled into a booth. He ordered our beers. "Did you miss me?"

"Of course. Did you miss me?"

"Sure." He looked away.

"You did it with someone else, didn't you?" *Well, of course he did. He was twenty-seven and owed me nothing.*

His face went red. "Well, sorta."

"What do you mean, sorta?"

"Okay. I did. Are you mad?"

"Mad? No. Why would I be mad? I don't own you." The waitress put down our beers and I took a drink. "As a matter of fact. So did I."

Tom nearly dropped his glass. "You did?"

"Don't be so surprised. It was you who started it."

"Started what?"

I smiled. "I would say, you started my whole new purpose in life. You woke up my barren lady parts and now they can't get enough of man parts."

"Well, damn it all. Good for you."

We clinked glasses.

"To sex," I said. "And more of it."

"So tell me about it. Who did you do it with and where?"

"A lady doesn't tell tales out of school."

"Fair enough. Just one thing. Was it someone from work?"

"Yes, both of them."

"Both!"

I laughed. "And on the same day. In your office. All week."

"In my office!"

"I was thinking of you the whole time."

He shook his head. "I have unleashed a beast."

"Yes, you have. Let's go somewhere and be bestial."

"I know just the place." He took my hand and, with our half finished beers sitting on the table, he led me along the hall toward the restrooms. We turned the corner and he stopped. He pushed me against the wall and slid his hand up my leg.

"What are you doing?"

"What do you think? I am having my way with you, you wicked lady."

"Not here. Someone might come by."

"That's what makes it so delicious." His hand slipped into my panties, over my bush and between my legs.

I opened them wider to let him in and with his fingers inside me, it didn't take me long to get wet. I wriggled against him, enjoying him feeling me. This was outrageous enough to be doing this in a public hallway but there was more to come.

He pulled his hand away, opened his fly and lifted my skirt. With a quick tug, my pants were down just far enough for his fully erect cock to find its place. We rocked together in perfect rhythm, moving faster with each thrust.

Footsteps sounded along the hall, and the closer they came, the closer he came. Just as the footsteps turned the corner, he finished with a grunt, pulled out of me and dropped my skirt. His back was to the woman as she walked by so she didn't see him tucking himself back into his pants. It looked as if we were just standing there talking.

"So how do you like your new job?" he said in a loud voice.

It seemed my new job was to keep Virginia happy while making a few men happy. "I love it," I said.

The woman went into the washroom and I reached down to pull my pants up.

"Let me help you do that."

He knelt down in front of me but instead of pulling my pants up, he pulled them down further and stuck his head under my skirt.

His tongue found a wet home and I gasped as it tickled my clitoris, starting sizzling to go up my thighs and stomach and back and—

I was groaning and squealing and yipping all at the same time, with my skirt covering Tom's head, and that's when the woman walked out of the washroom.

She smiled. "Lucky girl," she said as she passed.

I was too involved to be embarrassed. Tom was doing a masterful job with his tongue and soon another sweet and earth shaking orgasm rocked my world.

We took several minutes to recover and walked back to our table. Or beers were waiting.

The woman who had passed us sat two tables away. When she saw me looking at her, she gave me a thumbs up.

I had entered the wide and wonderful world of sex. Slow fucks or fast ones, with fingers, tongue or penis, I loved them all.

6: A New Start

I didn't ever think it would get tedious being with the same guy (or guys) all the time, but after a month of having weekday sex with Tom, Arnold and Jasper, I longed for something different. Once or twice I didn't even have an orgasm and that sucked. Well, maybe if I had been sucked it would have happened.

Tom, however, did add some spice to our sexual encounters. He loved the risk of public sex, and one early evening we went to the Central Library and in a far back corner in front of the Philosophy section we did it as quietly as we could. Another evening, we did it in the back row of a cinema. I don't remember the movie but it wasn't too crowded so we had the row to ourselves.

The fellow in front of us turned around and scowled, but when he saw what we were up to he didn't turn away. By the look on his face and how it got redder and redder, I am pretty sure he was busy with himself as he watched us. It added a new element having another man watch Tom bury his head under my skirt. What would it be like doing it with two men? *Oh, dear. What was I becoming?*

Once, we did it in a taxi in rush hour. The taxi driver kept glancing in the rear view mirror with a big smile on his face. And at a red light a bus stopped right beside us. A few shocked faces stared but I was too busy to care who was looking.

One warm evening, we were walking by the park and we ducked behind a lilac bush and did a stand up there.

The next time we did it was in an elevator. (He'd pushed the stop button at least.) When we reached the bottom floor and pushed through the crowd of waiting people, he said he had something important to tell me.

"What is it?" I said, doing up the top button of my blouse.

"I'm getting married."

"You're what?"

"I'm getting married."

"Does this mean—?"

"I promised her I would be a one woman man."

"Good luck on that one."

"It's not for another month, so we'll have time for some goodbye fucks."

The next few weeks were sweet, knowing he was soon going to be unavailable, but I was surprised that a part of me was glad. I was craving change. A new penis. New fingers inside me. New lips to lick me. A new man—or two —or three.

A week before his wedding, I handed in my resignation at Industrial Life. Jasper offered me a huge raise and new position. But the position he liked me in best was where he took me on the edge of the desk every day, face plunged in my bosom or between my legs.

When Arnold found out I was going, he looked as if he was about to cry.

"Arnold," I said. "You find yourself a nice girl and fuck her every day. She'll love it"

"Do you really think so?" He sniffed.

That afternoon, I introduced him to Susie, from reception. She was new, his age, and glad to have a friend. I told her what Arnold liked and she got the message. I was delighted that these young girls took to sex so easily. I had been born too early.

Next day, he was all smiles and I noticed they would disappear during break and come back looking like a pair of Cheshire cats.

On my last day at work, the girls gave me a little going away party. I had hooked up a few of the other younger ones with fellows from other floors, and I got a special thank you from them. It made me feel good to know that I was passing the pleasure around.

At 4:00 I had my final rendezvous in the boss's office. He cried harder and fucked harder than he ever had. Afterwards, he begged me set aside Tuesday nights for him, but I told him I didn't have a desk at home.

* * *

For a full week after leaving my job with its daily sexual dalliances, I lolled around the house, had baths, masturbated, and wondered what my next step would be.

I really liked sex, but didn't want a relationship. That was too complicated. I liked the slam bang, thank you ma'm type of sex, although I hadn't really experienced that. Something to look forward to.

After a week of male abstinence, Virginia was yearning for a nice big cock. Masturbating was okay, but along with the satisfying sex, I loved the anticipation of who and where and how it would be done.

I loved the feel of a big penis inside me, and a man's body thumping on me. I loved the smell of their sweat and the grunts they made. I loved it when they came, bursting inside me. But most of all, I loved the cartwheels and stars that exploded in my head. That feeling of being full, complete, and whole.

Reliving those delicious memories would last for a day, maybe half a day, before Ginny would start itching and prompting me to find a man. To be lifted off and taken to the moon.

On Monday, I signed up with a temp agency. I figured that would be a good way to meet more men, with different styles appendages, and without getting overly involved.

7: Mailman's Special Delivery

I had always found a man in uniform attractive. And that was before I had discovered the exquisite joys of sex. And so many men wore uniforms. Not just military, but policemen, firemen, mailmen. Hmm.

Where could I find a mailman? The Postoffice was removing more house deliveries and putting up those multiple boxes at the end of a street. Coincidentally (but I never believed in coincidences—surely the Universe was working on my side) on my first week at the temp agency, I was assigned a job at the main Post Office. It was only for three days, but long enough to find out which streets had mail delivery and which postmen did which ones.

I picked out the man first and made note of his route. After all, I didn't want to do it with just anyone. He was probably in his early forties. No ring on his finger so who knows how much sex he was getting. He had dark curly hair. Maybe Italian? Hmm. That sounds exciting.

His route was a residential one at the far end of town. The next day, I walked the route looking for a house I might somehow make use of. One for sale? An empty one? That wouldn't work if no mail was delivered. Then I spotted it. A three story rooming house with a sign in the window. Room for let. Perfect. (Thank you, Universe)

I walked up the pebble path and knocked on the door. No one answered so I went back in the early evening when a cheery middle-aged woman ushered me into the living room.

"Sit down, my dear. Let's have tea."

Over two flowered teacups and a matching teapot, she explained how her father had left her the rooming house and she loved to have the company.

When we finished our tea, she took me to a small room at the back on the third floor. The three doorways we passed on the second belonged to other tenants.

"They all work and are very quiet."

I was glad they worked. I needed privacy with my postman. "And do you work in the day?" I didn't want a busybody landlady nosing around.

"Oh, yes. I am out every morning at eight and back by five."

"I'll take it," I said.

The next day, I moved in with my one suitcase. I had explained I was just in town on business and needed a place for a short while. An older gentlemen lived in the room opposite mine, but I quickly found out, that except for meals, he only came downstairs at 4:00 p.m. when he went for a walk.

From working at the Post Office, I knew the mail delivery time, so next Monday at 3:00 I was waiting for my curly haired postman. He came bounding up the steps with a handful of mail but before he could slide it through the slot, I opened the door.

"Oh," he said. "You startled me."

"Sorry. I'm expecting a special delivery and I wondered if you had it for me?" I wore a light summer shirtwaist dress, full skirt with the top three buttons opened. As I spoke I slid my hand under the top part of my dress as if adjusting my bra strap. Would he get the message?

He glanced down at the letters. "What's your name?"

"Somerville—Miss." I usually used Ms. but Miss sent a clearer message.

He flipped through them. "Nope. Nothing today."

He handed me the letters. As I took them, I let my hand linger on his and then slid it slowly off. I looked him straight in the eyes and said, "Maybe tomorrow, you'll have a special delivery parcel just for me." Was he a dunce?

He blinked a couple of times, then stared at my opened blouse. "M-maybe." He turned and stumbled out.

I closed the door. It would be a long wait until tomorrow afternoon's delivery but it would be fun anticipating it.

At 4:00 o'clock, Charles, my neighbour across the hall, came tottering downstairs. He nodded to me as he went out.

He must be eighty but had a full head of snow white hair. Probably too old for sex. Too bad. Although I'd heard men never lose the desire.

The next day, I waited at the front door and precisely at 3:00, I opened it.

He scurried up the four wooden stairs and onto the veranda. "Hello, Miss Somerville."

"Hello there. Do you have special delivery for me today?"

"I think I might have a package for you." He was only holding letters and flyers, but the swell in his pants told another story.

"Come in." I opened the door wider.

He came in and closed the door behind him. The foyer was dimly lit. "Now, what is it you are expecting?" he said.

"What have you got?" I tilted my head. A little foreplay was fun and good to wet the appetite so to speak.

"I've got whatever you want." He dropped his mailbag on the floor, and his hand went to his belt buckle. He held it there for a moment and when I smiled, he flipped his belt open, and dropped his pants to the floor. "Something like this?" He put his hand into the flap in his shorts.

"Oh, yes. That package is exactly what I want." I lifted my full skirt. Today I had pants on. Sometimes men liked to pull them down. And that is what he did.

He stepped toward me, put his hands on each side of my waist and yanked. They slipped easily over my hips and in the next swift movement he pulled out a hard cock. I helped him find the entrance and grabbed his ass with both hands holding him against me. He banged and banged, harder and faster.

Breathlessly, between his delicious strokes, I encouraged him on, not that he needed it. "I like your delivery. Keep it coming Mailman. Keep it coming." And he certainly kept it coming and so did I until we both came together with a gush, nearly collapsing to the floor. He held on tight until we regained our footing, and grabbed a handkerchief from his pocket.

I pulled a hankie from under my bra strap and wiped the inside of my thigh where his milky cream dripped down. "That was quite a package."

"It has been growing since yesterday." He tucked himself in and pulled up his pants. He did his buckle up. "I will probably have another special delivery for you tomorrow?"

"That will be grand. I'll be waiting."

At dinner that evening, around the large dining room table, Mrs. Rushmore, the landlady, asked, "How are you making out, my dear?"

"Just fine, thank you. I think I'll like living here."

"I do hope so. Good tenants are hard to find."

Two sisters and a widow friend of Mrs. Rushmore lived on the second floor, so other than the old man opposite me, there didn't seem much chance of any extra curricular activities sexually wise. And I had little hope for the old man. But that was all right. My focus was on the mailman and that would be enough—for now.

Later, that night, I sat in front of the small mirror dresser and brushed my hair. Life was so good since I'd discovered sex. It was as if I hadn't lived before. I was glad I had no children to worry about or who might worry about me. And I was certainly glad I wasn't married. Variety was definitely the way to go.

There was a knock on my door. "Who is it?"

"Charles—from across the hall."

I opened the door. "Hello. What can I do for you." He was such a sweet old grandfather type in his plaid housecoat.

"May I come in for a moment?"

"Oh, sure."

He came in and closed the door.

"What can I do for you?" I said.

He held his hands together, and bent slightly over from the waist. "I started down early today for my walk."

What did that have to do with me? "Oh, yes. Did you have a nice walk?"

"Well, yes. Later I did. But you see, when I came down early, I stopped at the second landing and enjoyed watching the mailman give you his special delivery."

My mouth opened and I actually blushed. This man could be my father. "Oh, my. You weren't supposed to see that."

"I expected as much. But don't worry, my dear. I did so enjoy it."

What could I say? I waited. At least he wasn't offended.

"You seemed to like the interaction very much," he said.

"Yes, I did."

"I was wondering. . ." He trailed off.

"Yes?"

"Well, I know I'm an old man but my pecker still has life in it."

I opened my mouth again but no sound came out.

He continued. "Watching you and the mailman perked my pecker up. In fact, he's still pretty perky." He opened his bathrobe. He was naked and his cock shot up larger than life. Almost larger than his skinny thigh.

I closed my mouth. "How old are you?"

"Age doesn't matter, does it, my dear? My pecker is ageless."

"Well, blow me down. You just come right over here, old man." And I opened my robe. I too was naked.

I lay down on the bed and in two steps he lay on top of me.

"This is Heaven," he said, and put a soft but firm hand on each breast. "You have great tits. I like that word. Tits, tits, tits."

He squeezed and felt my tits like he hadn't been near any for years.

"I haven't done this for thirty years," he said.

"It's like riding a bicycle. You never forget." I picked up his swelling pecker and shoved it up me.

"There is a God in heaven," he said, pushing in and out with great gasps.

"Be careful. You might have a heart attack."

"Then I'll die happy," and he whooped like a cowboy on a bucking bronco.

The bed springs squeaked and I bounced with him as I was lifted up on huge wings into the stratosphere.

He came with a rush and a yell and stayed in me. "Have you come, my dear? In my day a gentleman always made sure his lady came too."

My space ship was still soaring and then it landed with a mighty crash on a planet far away. I cried, "Oh, yes, yes, yes. I have landed. That was a fine fuck."

"As good as the mailman?"

"Don't tell him, but it was better."

We lay side by side until we caught our breath. "I should go," he said.

"Why? No one else lives on this floor and it's a long night." I couldn't believe I was asking him to stay.

"All right," he said.

I pulled the sheet and quilt up over us. Sometime in the middle of the night I woke up with a fat cock inside me. Virginia was already awake and getting moist. It was slowly sliding in and out. No hurry. Just a lazy slow fuck while his hands kneaded my tits.

"Tits, tits, tits," he whispered.

I closed my eyes and pretended to be asleep. It was a challenge to hold my hips still. The tingle started and I wanted to take part in the climb to the heavenly hosts, but I would let him have his fun.

"Beautiful tits," he said between licking and sucking them, all the while slowly lifting himself in and out of me.

A delicious craziness enveloped me as my desire and passion built higher and higher. Just when I thought I couldn't stand it any longer, he started panting and moving more swiftly. Like a battering ram, his cock stayed inside, and his hands went under my bottom and moved me with him. I bit my tongue so I wouldn't cry out, and the dear old sexy codger fucked his brains out.

"Tits, ass, fuck, cunt, tits, fucking fucks," he muttered, voice rising higher as he came to the brink and flowed over. "Christ," he yelled and fell on top of me.

I wanted to yell with him, but kept quiet when Ginny came in a burst of starlight with him. Christ, indeed. I couldn't remember when I had been fucked so thoroughly.

He rolled off, breathing heavily. Then he leaned over and tenderly kissed each breast. "Thank you titties." Then he kissed my wet bush. "Thank you lovely cunt."

I never liked the 'c' word, but when he said it, it sounded so sweet and lovely.

The next morning he was gone—probably to sleep all day. I had a part time shift so I would be home by 2:30. At 3:00 I went downstairs to collect my daily mail. I was still satiated from Charles's amazing administrations last night, but I would do my best to rise to the occasion. At work that day I learned from Google that a woman's clitoris had the same nerve endings as a man's penis and actually rose up, just like a penis.

I must have an extra large one, because no matter how a man entered me, it always got tickled, rubbed and made alive which made sex so incredible. I wondered why I didn't have that with my late husband. Maybe my clitoris was hiding out and waiting for something else or maybe it grows with practice.

At 3:00 sharp, the mailman rushed in, dropped his bag and his pants. He lifted my skirt, pulled my pants down and pushed his special delivery in the right slot. Thoughts of Charles had already made me wet, so I was ready for the quick entrance. He banged against me, with little grunts on each thrust. One, two, three. Was Charles watching from the second floor landing? The thought of that made me come first and the mailman came right after me. He squeezed my buttocks hard and pulled out of me.

"How did you like that delivery?" he said.

Some men need assurance. "That was magnificent," I said. "And so quick."

He was still panting. "I have been thinking of this all morning and could hardly wait."

"Don't you have a girlfriend?"

"I'm between girlfriends so I go to a prostitute now and then, but you're better than them."

"Gee, thanks,"

"Oh, no offense. It's just that it's great to do it in a hallway on my mail route. Makes my job worthwhile."

"Are you up for another delivery tomorrow?"

"You betcha. Everyday. Forever."

He pulled up his pants, picked up his bag and turned to go. Then he turned back. "Can I feel your tits tomorrow?"

"I would like that. If you have time."

"Oh, yes. I can feel tits, and fuck at the same time." He tipped his hat, opened the door and left.

That evening, the plaid-robed Charles knocked at my door. Yes, he admitted. He had watched.

"How was it watching?'

"Exciting. Especially since I hoped I would be seeing you later."

"Did you masturbate while you were watching?'

"Charles Sr. insisted on having some attention."

"Charles Sr?"

"Now that my pecker is wide awake, he's the boss of me. I'll never be the same."

"Well, come to me," I said. "Virginia is awaiting the grand entrance of Charles Sr."

By the end of the week, I was exhausted. My part time job finished at 2:00 so I was ready for the mail at 3:00 but with at least two gigantic fucks every night, I needed a rest. The week ended and I decided to leave the boarding house that weekend. The mailman would be okay, but I hated leaving Charles with nowhere to put Charles Sr.

So I did some research and came up with a plan.

8: Never Too Old

After my last bedtime fuck with Charles, I said to him, "I'll be moving out tomorrow so this is our last night."

He sat right up. "Oh, no. You can't leave." He looked horror stricken.

"Don't worry, I have a plan for you."

"A plan."

"Yes, I wouldn't leave you fuckless. There's a seniors' retirement complex in the next town and there's a cottage available for you."

"But I can't afford that place. I'm only on a pension."

"Don't worry. I made a special arrangement for you with Mrs. Jenkins, the Manager."

"What arrangement?"

"When I told her about your special gift, Mrs. Jenkins, a widow, was most interested. And there are several other ladies who would be glad to meet Charles Sr."

"You mean—?"

"You just have to buy your food. Your rent is totally covered. All you have to do is leave your door unlocked every night."

"You mean—?"

"Every night a woman will tip toe in, come to your bed, ready and willing to meet Charles Sr."

His mouth dropped and his pecker rose. "Oh, my. Charles Sr. is certainly interested in that."

"Let's do it again to celebrate your new life."

He rolled on top of me and Charles Sr. had another rollicking good time. I was still hot and wet from his recent occupancy and lay back to enjoy another beautiful long fuck.

I'm going to jump ahead for a moment, because I just have to tell you how both Charlies made out.

Two months later, one sunny afternoon, I dropped in to the Senior's Residence to see how he was doing. He looked ten years younger and walked with a lively step.

"I am the happiest man alive. What a place. The women here are wild for sex."

"Tell me about it," I said, my vagina getting moist.

"Well, every night like you said, I leave my door unlocked. I sleep nude and sure enough a woman comes in and climbs into bed with me. Some of them are shy and it is fun coazing them, but some jump right on me. Some even like me to come in their mouth. I don't care where I put it. I do whatever they like to do or have me do to them."

"Tell me more." I wriggled on the settee opposite him.

"The great thing is, I don't know who it is that I fuck. The next day, when I pass a woman, we both smile politely. No one leers. No one lets on what's happening. And of course, I don't because I don't know who's come and who hasn't. I mean come to my room, not come in the other way. I make sure everyone of my lady friends come, if you get my meaning."

"I get your meaning." I hadn't come to see him for a fuck, but it was looking like I was going to have to get one.

"There's a plump one that's a real treat. It's like she's got four tits and she loves me to kiss and lick them all." He paused and smiled liked a goofy teenager. "Oh, yes. Charles Sr. is getting a fine work out." He giggled. "Last week, I had quite a challenge. Twins. Two sisters crawled under the covers. One sat on my face and let me put my tongue in her and the other one rode on my pecker. Then, with some hilarious gyrations, they managed to change places. Charles Sr. was certainly tired after that, but he always rallies to the occasion."

He reached across and touched my hand. "I can't thank you enough."

"I can think of a way for you to thank me." I spread my legs to show I was not wearing underpants.

"You never cease to amaze me, my dear. I will have to draw the blinds. I don't want any of my lady friends to know I do it in the day time. I would get no rest at all." He lowered the blinds and then lowered his pants.

Charles Sr. seemed bigger if that was possible.

He took my hand and led me to his bedroom. A handmade quilt, in a colorful array of blues and pinks and purples, covered the double bed.

"Mrs. Jenkins arranged for a larger sized bed for me." He folded the rainbow to the foot of the bed. "Several of the ladies in the quilting circle made it for me."

I lay down on the soft blanket and spread my legs. He took off his pants and I opened my blouse and let my tits loose. I knew he liked them. Charles Sr. found Virginia wet and waiting. He slid in easily and we had a grand time bouncing merrily until we both came. My tits bobbed up and down in his hands and he did his usual routine of quietly crying, "Tits, tits, titties. I love these babies," between licking, sucking, and squishing his head between them.

Afterward, dried and dressed, he said, "You always were the best. Anytime you need to be fucked, you just drop by, my dear. Anytime."

I have been busy with my other endeavours. Everywhere I turn, there seems to be another man waiting for a fuck, so I haven't been back. I imagine Charles, with his renewed interest in life and with Charles Sr.'s regained vigor, they'll be going strong till he's a hundred, pleasing a whole gang of lovely senior ladies who are finding retirement a bang up place.

9: The Fireman's Hose

Temp work was the best plan I ever had. Every single office I was assigned to had more than one frustrated man who could please me and I, them.

I picked them out easily and it didn't take much to let them know what I waned. I had already discovered that most men walk around with a hard on ninety percent of the time.

Board rooms were a great place for a rendezvous. Once we did it in the stair well and another time in a kitchen. Different places, different men. I loved the variety.

One day walking home from work, I passed a small fire that was being put out on an abandoned house. No one was hurt and the fireman were milling about, rolling up hoses and poking at smoking boards. I stopped for a look and stood on the sidelines. A young muscled fireman was holding a thick hose swelled with water.

"Okay, turn it off boys," came a shout from the truck.

A few final spurts, and the last drops dribbled out of his collapsing hose. The spot between my legs started twitching. I wanted that man's hose inside me. There was only a smattering of bystanders left, only a few stragglers watching.

The good looking fireman walked around the back of the truck which was parked close to the next building. That's when I made my move. I followed him and tapped him on the shoulder. He stopped screwing some kind of machinery on the truck and turned around.

"Are you all right ma'am. Can I help you?"

"Well, yes, you can."

"What can I do for you?"

"I was admiring your hose, especially when it was full." I slowly licked my lower lip. Corny, I know but it seemed to turn a switch in the male psyche.

His eyes got big. "Yes, we do have a big hose. That's for sure." His eyes bugged out more.

"I would love to see your big hose close up. Would that be possible?" I stepped closer.

"I think that can be arranged." He flipped open the clasps on his jacket and reached for those on his pants.

I had picked the right one. He looked about twenty-one and was hot. He scrambled through layers of jacket to get to his pants. Then through outer pants, and inner pants. Finally, a zip and there it was—a good long full and erect hose pointing at me.

I stepped up to him and lifted my skirt. I was wearing my new pants with the snap crotch and with a quick flip I opened the flap. He took my shoulders in his two hands and leaned me against the truck. Then he held his penis in one hand and with the other hand behind my backside, snaked his hose to where it fit perfectly.

The shouts of firemen from the other side of the truck, heightened our urgency. Footsteps headed our way but my fireman kept thumping against me. The footsteps were coming and so were we. Just when they were almost upon us, a shout called him back.

My randy fire fighter finished with a bang and pulled out of me, leaving stars flashing inside my head. He did up his clothes while I held onto the truck in a stupor. There was nothing better than this. I could die happy right now.

"So what do you think of a fireman's hose?" he said.

His words were dim and far away, but I caught the gist. Men liked to be acknowledged. "I love your hose," I said dreamily. "So big and strong."

10: The Board Room

I had flexibility with the Temp Agency and it paid the bills. I could take a day off when and if I needed it. With my riveting sexual pastime, I couldn't have held a steady job anyway. I made a point of not approaching men in my building and I never brought any home to my apartment. Tom was the only one who had been there.

Sometimes, after a rousing session, a man would slip a couple of bills inside the waistband of my pants or if I didn't have any pants on on a nearby desk, or filing cabinet. At first, I was affronted. After all I wasn't a prostitute. But then, I thought, what the hell, if it made them feel better, so be it. I could always use some extra cash. And it did put a different spin on my encounters to pretend I was a lady of the night. Hmm. That might be fun to initiate.

The temporary work at offices also supplied a fresh batch of men. As I said, most office men were uptight and sexually frustrated so it wasn't difficult to find willing subjects. The bosses liked it when I offered to work late and some offices had couches which was more comfortable than desk tops or stuffy mail rooms.

One time I did it in the board room on an oversized oak table. Josh Jenkins, one of the bosses, in his early forties, reminded me of Tom a little. Handsome and a good body. I had eyed him on my first day of work. In three days, I was "promoted" to be his private "girl." Not that I could officially be promoted, but since I was a temp I went where I was told, and when the boss said he wanted me for extra help, I happily complied. The next day he asked if I could stay late. Catching the glimmer in his eyes, I pretended to be coy.

"I guess I could manage that." I said, glancing at his bulging pants.

I didn't wear plunging necklines or tight clothes. I didn't have too. Somehow men smelled me out as a sexual creature.

That day, I had on my usual office wear—a straight grey skirt, black pumps, and a white tailored blouse. Very business like.

Everyone had left and I was typing on the computer when Mr. Jenkins called me into his office.

"Have you finished the report, Ms. Somerville?"

"Yes, sir. Here it is." I handed him the paper. His hand covered mine as he took it. I pulled my hand away with a little blush. *Let him have his fun*.

"Do you enjoy working here, Ms. Somerville?"

"Oh, yes sir. I do."

He looked at a folder on his desk and then looked up. "Do you mind if I call you Sherry?"

"I would like that, sir."

"And you don't have to call me sir. Call me Josh."

"All right—Josh." I looked coyly away. How long was this going to take?

"Would you like a small drink of something. I do appreciate you staying late to finish the report."

"That would be nice."

He went to an oak cabinet, took out a bottle and two glasses. "Have you seen the board room?" he asked.

"No, I haven't. Is it a big room?"

"Oh, yes, very big with a big table."

I hoped something else was getting big.

He filled my glass and handed it to me. "Come this way, I'll show it to you."

It's about time. I followed him down a long hall to a set of carved doors. He pushed one open and flicked on the light. A sixteen foot oak table crowded the room with seven chairs lined along each side. An ornate throne chair sat at the front.

"That's a fancy chair," I said.

"Would you like to try it?"

"I'd love to." And try you too.)

I put my glass on the table and lowered myself into it the huge chair. Placing my hands on the upholstered arms, I said, "Feels nice." When was he going to start?)

"You're a very attractive woman, Sherry."

"Thank you, Josh."

"Do you find me attractive?"

"Yes, I like younger men."

"And I find mature woman fascinating."

He stood over me, his zipper near my face. I hoped he didn't just want a blow job. I like to pleasure men, but I want to be pleasured while doing it. I stood up, putting my face about two inches away from his. His hot and panting breath warmed my cheeks. Without a word, he rolled the throne chair out of the way and lifted me up to the edge of the table. He slid his hands down over my hips and then reached up under my skirt. We were looking into each others eyes as he did it. I neither objected nor encouraged him.

My skirt was too tight for him to get to the top of my pants, so he pulled his hands out and went to the zipper on my skirt. He slid it open, pushed my skirt down and lifted my bottom to take it all the way off. It fell to the floor. Next came my panty hose. Still gazing at me and I, at him, he slowly rolled them down. It wasn't a staring contest. We both blinked now and then. It was two people watching and anticipating a delicious coming event. The panty hose was off, along with my shoes. He moved his hands over the top of my silk panties, over my bottom and around my hips as if looking for the entrance.

My roller coaster started to climb. He would have to hurry. I could barely hold his eyes as I willed him to get on with it. Finally, he slipped his fingers into the top band of my panties and inched them down, over my hips, over my bottom. Then he lifted me and they were down to my thighs. He stopped. Take them right off, I screamed inside.

His gaze left my face and went to my crotch. He stared and rubbed a hand over my pubic hair. Okay, if he didn't want to use his penis, start with the fingers, but do something. My roller coaster rose higher and higher. I reached for his zipper. He didn't object. I pulled it down and while I did that he slid my pants down and off my feet. Still he stood there. Was I going to have to do everything? I reached inside his pants. His member was big and hard. I pulled it out. His penis popped free and came right to the table edge and me. I guided it to the place that had been waiting all day.

His hands held my bottom as he slid in and out. On and off the table I slid with him inside me. Faster and furiouser, climbing to the top. We reached together and I flew into the outer regions of the atmosphere. To Nirvana. I didn't know how long we stayed stuck together. It felt like eternity, but finally he pulled out of me. I felt drunk, and not from alcohol.

He tucked himself back into his pants, zipped up and bent down and put my skirt, pantyhose and underpants on the table beside me. Then, without a word, he turned and left the room.

I lay back on the table, naked from the waist down, my hands cupped between my legs, holding the pleasure in. Stars swirled around, white light encircled me. I stayed in wonderland for a good long while.

Finally I got dressed and went to the cloak room for my coat. There was only the janitor sweeping up.

"Good night, Ms. Somerville," he said.

"Good night." How did he know my name?

I worked at that company for another week. Every night Josh had an important report for me to finish, so I had to work late. And each night he would offer me a drink. Each night we would pretend anew and act out the same scenario as if for the first time.

It was nice to know that sex would be the ending of every work day. It took the pressure off finding someone.

I could have gone on longer with him, but on Friday a smartly tailored woman by the name of Mrs. Josh Jenkins arrived at 5:00 p.m. Josh seemed surprised and he cancelled the report that he had ordered earlier from me. The next morning, I had been transferred to another floor.

11: Brooms, Mops, and other Long Sticks

The next day I got settled into my new position on the floor below Josh's office. I knew there would be no more dalliances with him so I scanned the area. I was in an office pool full of women. Tough luck. Where were the men?

At the end of work, I closed my computer and walked out with the other "girls." As we walked through the hall, we passed the janitor.

He smiled and waved. "Good night, ladies."

One girl leancd over and whispered, "Watch out for him. He's a randy old bugger."

"What do you mean?" I said in mock horror, covering my tingle of hope.

"If you work late, he'll try to lure you into his broom closet."

"Oh, dear. Has he ever succeeded?"

"Are you kidding? I hear he's hung like a race horse. Greek, I think. Pity the poor women he gets his hands on."

My twat was getting wet just thinking of it. but I said, demurely "Oh, my. Thank you so much for telling me. I will be careful." Yes, I'll be careful to work late tomorrow.

The next morning, I dressed carefully. I deliberated whether to wear my panties with the snap crotch or no pants or my slippy silk ones. He might be one who likes to rip them off. I decided on a pair of easy-to-rip cotton ones.

All day I wriggled in my chair just thinking of meeting up with "Randy Andy" in the hall. No one knew his name and what's in a name anyway.

At five, we closed our computers and picked up our purses. I walked out with the girls, but just as we got to the elevators, I patted my purse. "Oh, I forgot something. You go ahead. I'll see you tomorrow."

They waved goodbye and I went back to the pool room, with rows of desks. I went to mine, and pretended to search in the drawers while the last stragglers left. When everyone was gone, I waited another five minutes.

I walked into the hall. Empty. I lingered by the doorway for a moment. At the far end of the hall, a figure appeared pushing a cart. Brooms and mops, stuck out. It came closer.

I started walking slowly toward the elevators which also happened to be toward the cart which was moving closer and closer to me.

He stopped. "Is that you Ms. Somerville?"

"Yes."

"Late leaving?" He pushed the cart forward.

"Yes."

He reached me. "Nice evening."

"Yes."

"My name's Tony."

"My name's Sherry."

"That's a pretty name."

"Yes."

"Are you working on this floor now?"

"Yes."

"I guess you don't see Mr. Jenkins anymore."

"Not anymore."

He had stepped out from behind the cart and the front of his pants strained to hold the bulge back. "That's too bad. I hear he liked seeing you."

I lifted my eyebrows. "What do you mean?"

"The walls to the boardroom are thin and I have very good hearing."

"Oh dear. What must you think of me?"

"I think you'd really like to visit my broom closet." He turned the cart around. "Are you coming?"

Very soon, I hoped. "I've never been to a broom closet."

I followed him along the hall, hoping no one else was working late and would suddenly come out. We got to the end of the hall. He pushed the cart to the side and opened a door. I stepped in. It was more of a room than a closet.

Cupboards lined each side of the entrance holding cleaning supplies, but it opened up at the back where a table and chair stood. A side table held a kettle and a lunch box. Beside the table was a small couch with a tiny TV in front of it.

"This is quite the layout," I said.

"All the comforts of home. Well, most of them. My wife never comes here."

"Your wife?"

"I like to be honest with people." The bulge in his pants was begging to be released.

"I do too." I put my purse down, took off my jacket and tossed it on the couch.

He walked up to me, pulled my skirt up and yanked my pants down. In the next second his huge cock was flying free and searching for a home. He didn't take long to find it. I was already moist and ready for him, but when he started pushing it in me, I gasped. Was it going to fit? He gently, but firmly slid in and out, in and out, each time getting in further.

His eyes were closed and his hands grasped my bare bottom pulling me to him with each thrust. My knees were getting weak and still inside me he lifted me to the couch one step away. He laid me down, my skirt bunched around my waist and not loosing stroke he continued with his task.

Kneeling astride me, he banged up and down, his huge battering ram filling every inch of Virginia. She had never been so full and so excited. I had heard the phrase, 'fucking your brains out' and now I knew what it meant. My head was swimming as I bounced in rhythm with him, climbing the roller coaster to ecstasy.

With a cry of "Jesus, Holy Mother of God," he came with a woosh and collapsed on top of me. I had reached my own pinnacle and lay like a rag doll under him.

I don't know how long it was before either of us moved but when he pulled out of me, I thought he was taking half of me with him. He grabbed a cloth from the back of the couch. "I must say Ms. Somerville. That was some fuck."

"Please call me Sherry."

"Thank you for the pleasure, Sherry."

"Thank you—Tony." I nearly forgot his name.

"Will you be working late tomorrow?"

"I—I'm not sure. I might need a day's rest."

He laughed. "I've heard that before. My wife can only take it three times a week so she doesn't mind my having extras

at work."

I wobble out of there still in a daze. The next morning I called in sick. Poor Virginia was so sore I could hardly walk. The next day I left at five with the girls. I mean a girl can only take so much. Even this one.

That evening my temp service phoned with another assignment. I wasn't sad. One time with Tony was enough. However, I might text Jennifer who sat beside me in the typing pool and tell her where she could get a gigantic fuck

My next week was uneventful in the sex department and it was kinda nice to day some time off. After all there was more to life than sex wasn't there? Only kidding. right now, for me, life was sex.

So many men in the world. And each one of them carrying a delicious package in their pants. Most of them panting to get out and get it in somewhere. That's the part that I loved about them. The part that would send me into orbit and reconnect me with All That Is.

I lived for that moment of climax, of feeling connected. It didn't matter which man pounded on top of me. What mattered was the joining to my whole self, to who I really was. It was only then I felt complete. It wasn't quite the same when I stimulated myself. It was pleasurable but I never reached the heights that I did with a man in me. Sometimes pleasuring myself would leave me frustrated and discontent and I'd be driven to search for another penis to plunge on top of.

Fortunately, most men's attention were on that part of their body so it didn't take much to have them drop their pants.

And drop them they did. Over the next months, I did it in elevators, I did it in airports, I did it in dark corners of bars, I even did it once while eating at a table in a restaurant. Okay, that one was a finger fuck but the table cloth was long and so were his fingers. I honestly had no idea of sex when the gentleman asked if he could sit at my table. I nodded and he sat beside me. I had already had a morning sex, so I wasn't looking for any at that moment. I was enjoying my piece of cherry pie when a hand touch my thigh. It rested there for a few seconds and then started bunching up my skirt.

He looked at me innocently as he reached skin. "Nice day."

I took another fork full of pie. "Very nice," I said just as innocently.

The hand kept moving. I spread my legs. Two fat, long fingers reached my crotch, crawled into my pants, into me and had a fine time playing there. They wriggled around, and slid in and out. I had to stop myself from crying out on each thrust, as I climbed higher and higher. He finished me with a bang, just as I finished the last bite of cherry pie.

He smiled and got up."Have a nice day."

I smiled back. "I just did."

Living in Canada meant that in the summer, it was easier. Men took me behind bushes in the park, behind statues, under bridges, and at the Canadian National

Exhibition behind the Arts and Crafts building. Certainly a lovely summer past time.

My longest sojourn of fucking with the same man was with Tom. (Other than my husband. However, I wasn't awake of what sex could be like then. But after Tom, I preferred one night stands with no emotional entanglement. My only goal was to be brought to that overflowing point of smashing through to that place of wholeness and spiritual communication.

Once a man was finished, I didn't want him to linger. I was glad when it was a quickie. I didn't want cuddling, I didn't want conversation or a cigarette.

I just wanted him to go, so I could lay in the aftermath of that sweet feeling of belonging to the Universe. It was as if God had fucked me. Maybe he had. I wondered if God had a penis.

Some men were rough. I didn't like that. One man at a party grabbed me and took me upstairs and with a sleazy leer said he was going to have his way with me. When I smiled and lifted my skirt and started to pull my pants down, he ran away. He didn't want to do it unless he forced me. What was that all about?

Violent sex wasn't sex, it was pure violence and I had nothing to do with such sickies. Sure, I loved strong men on me and in me. I loved it when they grabbed my bum and rammed me to them.

I lowered my skirt, got off the bed and went downstairs. Right away. I spied a shy man in a corner and after a five minute conversation with him led him upstairs to a coat-covered bed. It didn't take too much coaxing to rouse his natural impulse. t was fun doing it on a fur coat. Felt kind of primitive as if we were animals in a cave.

And he was rather wild. Sometime the shy ones surprise you. He surprised me twice after only a short break between.

13: Enlightening a Neighbour

Coming up in the elevator, last week, my neighbour, Julia, from the apartment down the hall, commented on the frequency and variety of my men friends. I must have let a few names slip, because I never brought any of them home.

She asked. "Do you have sex with them?"

"I like sex. There's no harm in that is there?"

"But what about morals?"

"What do you mean morals? I'm not married. There's no law against having sex is there? And they never pay me, so I'm not a prostitute."

"But—"

"It's more fun giving it away. You should see the look on their faces when I lift my skirt and I have no pants on."

Her mouth opened. "You're shameless."

But she kind of half smiled, and I said, "You should try it some time."

"Oh, I couldn't. I've only known one man in that way, and now he's gone. God rest his soul."

"So how was sex with him."

The elevator opened on our floor and we walked along the corridor. "Okay, I guess," she said. "I never had any comparison. After three kids, things changed."

"Do you pleasure yourself?"

"What do you mean?"

"You know. Masturbate."

Her face turned red. "I could never do that. It's a sin."

"Julie! Whoever said that must be a sick, defeated and half-dead person. Is it a sin to wash yourself, to feed yourself, to love yourself?"

"Well, no."

"It's the same thing. Next time you have a bath or shower, give yourself a feel down there. You might be surprised."

"I have to go," she said and hurried to her doorway.

The next day, I saw her again. We came up in the elevator but there were a sweet old couple with us. They got off on the floor before ours, and when the door shut I said. "So did you try it?"

"Try what?"

"Oh, Julie. Don't be coy. Did you give yourself a thrill?"

We got off the elevator and walked a few steps before she answered. "I fumbled around looking for the sweet spot."

"Good for you girl. Did you find it?"

A big smile. "I sure did. Glory be. Thank you, Sherry. I never realized so much pleasure was sitting there between my legs."

"You're welcome."

We went into our apartments. It's so nice to help out a neighbour.

14: Hat Trick

Was there a thrill in the danger? Or was it the thrill I got when a man became excited at my willingness. Some of them liked the hunt, so I would play hard to get. As long as we finally did it. One night I did it three times with three different men. That was a record for me. I had checked into a hotel that had advertised an insurance convention. Those men were uptight and like first year college students would rip loose given a chance.

First, I picked a distinguished older man with a full head of white hair. He stood tall and strong and looked vital. I winked at him and tilted my head toward the door. He lifted his eyebrows, looked both ways, and followed me out.

When we got to my room he said, "Are you a prostitute, because I'm not paying for it."

"Don't insult me. Of course, I'm not a prostitute. I just like sex. But if you don't want to—" I moved toward the door. "That's okay."

"Oh, no," he said, and pulled off his suit jacket and fumbled with the knot of his grey silk tie. "I'm delighted you like sex. I like it too. I wished my wife liked it more."

"You're married."

"Yes, that's okay, isn't it?"

"That's fine. Most married men know what to do." I stepped out of my shoes, lifted my skirt, and pulled my panty hose and pants all the way off.

By now he had his shirt off. A soft round belly pushed against an undershirt. He started to take that off.

"Why don't you keep that on," I said, and I lay down on the bed with my skirt pulled up to my waist.

"Aren't you going to take your dress off?" He undid his belt buckle.

"Everything you need is down there." I had hiked my skirt up at the back so it wouldn't get soiled.

"You are a strange women." He pulled his trousers down and stepped out of his shoes.

"Is it strange to want sex?"

"Some women think so." He removed his boxer shorts and with his member rising to the task he came to the side of the bed.

"What kind of foreplay do you want?" he said.

How considerate. He must make his wife happy. "I don't need any foreplay. I like to get right to the play." I spread my legs and curled my fingers to beckon him.

"Okay." And he straddled me. "This is great. I can't believe this is happening." He quickly stuffed his penis in, and huffing and puffing he pushed up and down. I smashed my hips into him, reaching for the moment, coaxing my body into ecstasy. It didn't take long and my roller coaster turned on. It climbed higher and higher. Up and up it crawled, as he grunted on top of me. Almost there, almost, yes, I'm coming. I'm coming. Then I hit the top and exploded in a nebula of attachment. I was one. I was whole. I was alive.

Half aware of him rolling off and getting dressed, I lay in bliss. He pulled my skirt demurely over me when he finished. I wouldn't move now for over an hour. Some men thought I had fallen asleep. Sometimes I did. Sometimes that circle of satisfaction would swirl me into sleep and when I awoke in the morning, I would feel satiated and able to function for a day or two, until I need another sex fix.

That night, however, with just a little rest and the lure of so many available men nearby and the anonymity of the hotel room, I felt the urge rising in me again. I picked up my panty hose and pants and laid them on the chair. I slipped into my low pumps and went downstairs. I mingled and set my eyes to finding a willing partner. Who was I kidding? Every man was willing, given a chance. That's what made this sex game so easy. I spied a fellow standing alone by the bar. He was younger, probably early forties, and wore black horn rimmed glasses. His straight black hair, which matched his glasses, flopped over his forehead.

I walked up to the bar, got a glass of white wine and turned to him.

"So what do you do in insurance?" I asked.

"Actuaries, actually." He smiled awkwardly.

This was a shy one. This should be fun. Should I be gentle or bold? What the heck. Let's go for bold. I stepped close to him and let my hand brush over his crotch. "And what actually are actuaries?" His pants moved instantly.

"Oh, my—they—er. Well—actually—"

I was now stroking my hand over the front of his pants and getting a good response. My body shielded what I was doing from others, but he certainly felt it. "I have a room upstairs," I said. "Would you like to tell me about it up there?" I gave him a little squeeze.

"Oh, my. Well—yes.I would actually like that—very much."

He stumbled out with me, babbling about life expectancy tables and flowsheets. We were alone in the elevator and just for fun I lifted my skirt. I was bare underneath and his mouth dropped. I took one of his hands and placed it between my legs. He froze. I started to wiggle onto his fingers, but the ding of the elevator told us we had reached my floor. I just got my skirt down and his hand out when the doors opened and a trio of noisy drinkers crowded on. My companion and I squeezed past them to get out.

In my room, the poor man was beside himself, hopping awkwardly on one foot trying to take his shoe off. He repeated his little dance with the other shoe and after a few tortuous moments of finding snaps and buttons, got his pants down. Meanwhile, I lay on the bed, my skirt up to my waist and my hands interlaced behind my head.

He kept his glasses on and pulled his Maple Leaf boxer shorts down and stepped out of them. His penis swelled to greater heights and I smiled. This would be a good one. He fell onto and into me, filling me to the brim. We rocked and rocked as my familiar roller coaster climbed to its highest summit and to a fiery finish.

He stayed inside me, panting and when he did pull out and get off me, he straighten his glasses and said, "Thank you, thank you, thank you."

"My pleasure," I said.

He got dressed while I lay there, still bare from the waist down. My lower extremities pulsing with life and energy and completeness. I was one again with all. I closed my eyes and didn't hear him leave.

About an hour later, I rose and checked the time. Midnight. The witching hour. I couldn't believe that my body wanted more of the delicious feeding after already having two fucks that night. I may as well make it a hat trick and make good use of the hotel room and the bevy of men below.

I had brought a small overnight case and a change of clothes in case of mishaps. The black sheath was an old reliable. Yoga exercises helped me with endurance and flexibility but I still retained my soft curves that men liked. Some women fought to lose those twenty pounds that the charts said were overweight but I never minded them. A pillow for men's boney parts to lean into or rest on.

I slid into the black dress. Its sheer sleeves fluttered like butterfly wings as I brushed my hair. One more time tonight. Was I a sex addict? Well, it was healthier than smoking or drinking, although I did like the odd glass of red wine.

Downstairs, I surveyed the room. The party was in full blast. Along with the steady clink of glasses, the laughter and loud voices attested to the releasing of office protocol and dreary rules. Probably most of the men and women were from out of town and what happened out of town, stayed out of town. I looked around, my antennae scanning for a willing man. It was easy. Every man was willing and eager. I felt a tap on my shoulder and turned around.

"Excuse me, madam. My friend told me you have special talents."

"Oh, and what would that be?"

He put both his hands on my behind and pulled me gently to him, pressing me against his hardness.

My crotch lit up and begged for this man to do it. "Your friend is right."

"Come with me," he said.

I smiled. I look forward coming with you.

He put an arm around my shoulders and led me to the balcony. The night air was balmy and the city lights glittered beyond. There were several cement benches with large plotted plants between them. He led me behind a large ficus and pulled my straight black skirt up my legs, over my hips and to my waist. No underpants. No panty hose. A clear field prepared and waiting. He opened his fly and, sliding his shirt tail aside, found a willing penis to do his bidding.

He didn't need direction or help, and with the sound of laughter spilling from the crowded room, he entered my wet doorway and into my deep recesses.

His sure and rapid strokes carried me higher and higher. My ready roller coaster, moved closer to flying off the rails where I would be thrown into space to never return.

"Don't stop," I panted.

"Don't worry. I won't." He panted harder.

The heavens exploded. The stars swirled. The planets wobbled and space erupted. After that, complete silence. No breath. No life.

Nothing except the fullness of everything. We stood for a long time, glued together, regaining our breath and our identity.

When he pulled out of me, I gasped and teetered off balance. He held me steady and then he tucked his penis away and zipped up.

I pulled my dress down and we returned to the party. I didn't stay. I sailed to my room in a cloud of mystery. Took off my dress and bra and lay on the bed. A nude Eve, in the aftermath of making love to the Universe, and drifted into a euphoric sleep.

15: Do it Again, Sam

One slow Sunday I went to the mall and popped in and out of shops. In the Unisex store, a young woman clerk brushed by me, lightly touching the front of my blouse. Hmmm. I'd never tried it with a woman. Something to think about.

Hallmark cards was right next door so in I went and soon found a young man who took me into the back room where he cared enough to give his very best.

It wasn't the best for me, however. First I stopped into the food court and got a bite. Just a bite of food. It was crowded with lots of kids, so I finished my tea and remembered the music store.

It had offered good finds in the past where hot young fellows hung out and there was a small storeroom in the back where supplies were kept. Mostly it was shelves with boxes of CD's and DVD's, but enough room for a stand up fuck.

I hastened over. Three customers were flipping through titles, and two fellows stood at the cash register. I studied them for a moment and picked the stocky blond one who looked like an ex-hockey player.

I walked over. "Could you help me find a CD?"

"Certainly, ma'am." He smiled his usual 'greet a customer smile'.

Shit. I'm a ma'am. Oh, well. Maybe he's got a mother obsession. "I forget the name of it, but it goes like this." I hummed a little tune.

"Don't recognize that one. What's the name of the artist?"

"Something like Big Dick." I said with a straight face.

He laughed. "Never heard of that one."

I slowly traced a wet tongue over my lower lip. "Maybe it's in the back room?" I tilted my head, letting my hair swish over my face for a moment before I tossed it back.

He stared at me and his eyes grew larger. "Oh, I see. Now that I think of it, I'm pretty sure the Big Dick is definitely in the storeroom."

"Splendid."

"This way, Ma'am. I'm sure we'll find it."

I followed him to the back and into the small room. With no door, the sounds of customers could easily be heard and it was possible that one of them or the other clerk might walk by any minute. After the woman in the clothes store had touched my breast, I had gone into the washroom and removed my pants but then chickened out going back to her store to see what might develop.

The blond ex-hockey player and I squeezed between the row of shelves. There was barely room for the two of us to face each other. He said in a loud voice, "Let's see if we can find what you want."

"Oh, I am sure it's here," I said just as loudly.

He lifted my skirt and when his hands touched my naked thigh and my behind, he gasped. His large hands cupped my buttocks and squeezed and patted and rubbed them like he was kneading bread. His pants filled in front and pressed against me.

While he massaged my bum, I unzipped him and pulled out what I wanted. Another gasp escaped from him as I wriggled myself on top of his big dick. He bucked against me and a pile of CD's fell off the shelf.

With a strong steady rhythm, his hands pulled my bottom to him. Slap, slap, slap, we bounced, knocking more CD's down over our shoulders.

The other clerk poked his head through the doorway. "Hey, Sam. Are you allri—Oh my God!" He turned around, framing the door with his body.

"What's going on in there?" said a woman customer. She tilted her head, trying to see over the clerk's shoulder.

"Must be a squirrel making all that ruckus."

"A squirrel?" she said. "However would a squirrel get in there?"

"Oh, they have their ways. Sam is dealing with it. No problem." Another crash. More CD's tumbled down, and then quiet.

"I think Sam got it handled. Can I help you with something?" He led the curious customer away.

We tidied our clothes and left the storeroom.

"Sorry I couldn't find the CD you wanted," Sam said.

"Oh, I am quite satisfied with what you found. Perhaps I'll come another day and we can search for Big Dick again."

"That would be fine, Ma'am. Just fine."

I left the store. He could call me Ma'am all he wanted as long as he gave it to me. With Virginia satisfied, I headed home for a cup of herbal tea. I did so enjoy a soothing drink after sex. Much better than a cigarette. Although I've never smoked, so what do I know?

I cuddled up in my favourite chair and relived those crashing moments with CD's falling over our heads. I moved my mug to my left hand and slid my dominant right hand up under my skirt and between my legs. In less than a moment, I was squirming against my fingers, feeling Sam's big dick inside me and living the pleasure all over again.

That night in bed, I thought there was no better activity in all the world than sex.

Another visit or two at the music store was definitely part of future plans.

16: Picture Perfect

Next Tuesday, after a dull day at Majestic Lighting with no opportunities rising, I went back to the mall. I strolled by the picture booth where those four instant snapshots are taken, and thought that would be a good place to have sex. I would just have to find a man to take in with me.

I sat on a nearby bench watching people pass. Several men looked at me, one or two looked twice but didn't come back. I couldn't be too forward or people would think I was a prostitute, although I was careful to not dress like one. That day I wore a print dress, with a shirtwaist collar, like any ordinary housewife. After my sexual awakening, I had coloured the gray streaks in my hair and joined a Pilates class to keep fit for my new pastime.

As I was thinking of a way to approach someone, a man sat down beside me and opened a newspaper. He wore an open sports shirt and kaki pants. Blond and clean looking. Probably early fifties. He looked delicious. The weather was always a good opening line, but before I could say a word he put his paper down and spoke.

"I wonder if you could do a favour for me?" he said.

"What's that?"

"I need to have my picture taken with a woman. My mother wants me to get a girl friend and I would really like to send her a picture. It would make her happy and keep her quiet."

"Oh, you mean in the picture booth over there?" Was it that easy?

"Yes, it won't take long."

"Well, yes, I guess I could do that."

We walked to the booth and sat side by side on the little bench. He pulled the half curtain shut, our legs showing beneath. He put in the coins.

"What do we do?" I said.

"We just sit here and smile." He clicked the button and we smiled and tilted our heads toward each other, like girlfriend and boyfriend.

"Thank you very much." He made a move to get up.

Wait. "Do you want to do more?" I asked.

"You mean more pictures?"

"Maybe there's something else we could do in here?" I smiled my best "come hither" smile.

His eyes flickered and his mouth curved upwards. "I'm sure we could think of something."

My bare crotch twitched. "There's not much room."

"Why don't you sit on my lap—facing me." I turned and swung one leg over him. I was glad I followed my intuition that morning and put on a full skirt. His throbbing lump in his pants pressed against me.

"This is nice," he said. "Where do we go from here?"

He was such a gentleman, letting me take the lead.

I lifted my skirt, exposing my pubic hair and forthcoming lady parts. He took in a sharp breath, and unzipped his pants. His penis struggled to be free of his underpants, while my crotch tingled in anticipation.

In a flash he thrust his eager staff into me and I rode him like a wild woman.

We were well into it—well, in and out very rapidly— when a knock sounded on the side of the booth. "Are you two finished in there?" came a woman's voice.

"Just about," my valiant warrior croaked, and with that he came with a woosh.

I hit the top of my crescent and bit my lip to stop from screaming. I grabbed a handful of tissue from my top pocket and mopped up. He zipped up and I climbed off.

We slid the curtain open, walked around the booth, and retrieved the strip of innocent pictures. They were perfect.

"Thank you," he said. "It was an unexpected delight having my picture taken with you. My mother will be pleased."

He went over to the bench, picked up his newspaper and walked away.

I stared at him as his well rounded behind disappeared into the crowd. My body still sizzled. Damn it, sex was good.

17: A Crowded Elevator

Elevators offer an intriguing slice of life— daring and public—and I particularly love it when they are crowded. I could secretly reach around in the crowd and slip my hand on the front of a man's pants, and feel him get hard. I always kept my face tilted up, staring at the flashing floor numbers with an innocent look.

Some men glanced around, but I kept my gaze averted. Sometimes, it was difficult to tell the gay men from the straight. But the gay guys were great sports. They would laugh and let me have a feel. However, feeling men up in elevators usually didn't lead to a good fuck, but one could always hope. And one day it happened. It was my first day at Laser Computers, on the 56th floor. It would be a long ride up, so I might as well have some fun.

People crammed into the elevator, some balancing a coffee, others holding briefcases. The odd, "sorry" or "excuse me" sounded as people pushed into each other. Perfect. I was stuck in the middle, bodies pressing all around me. Should I reach sideways or behind? It was a risk grabbing behind because I didn't want to latch onto a woman. I dropped my hand and brushed against a pant leg and the bottom of a man's suit jacket. Then I moved my hand over and cupped it between his legs. He grew harder and harder as I moved my hand over him. The elevator stopped and some people got out. I stayed pressed against him. It was still crowded enough. But at each stop the elevator emptied more until I had to drop my hand and step away. On floor 30 there were ten people left, by floor 40 only five and by my floor, only I and the man behind me. I had not turned around. What or who had I grabbed?

The light for 56 flashed, and the man stepped forward and hit the hold button. He placed his briefcase on the floor and turned to face me. Tall, well tailored blue suit, wrinkled at the crotch, trim mustache, grey hair, maybe sixty years old.

"Big crowd today," he said.

"Yes, quite."

"Would you like to see what you were feeling?"

He unbuttoned his jacket and put his fingers on the top of his zipper.

"That would be my pleasure, but only if I show you mine."

"Absolutely."

He undid his zipper and pulled out an erect penis.

I lifted my skirt, and pulled my pants down to my ankles. I stepped out of them as he moved toward me. I was already wet when he entered me. He pushed me to the back of the elevator and lifted me up as wrapped my legs around him and rode him. It didn't take long. He came first but kept inside me, moving back and forth and around until I came.

I found my pants and put them on as he straightened his clothes. "Are you getting off on this floor?" he asked.

I grinned at his choice of words. "Yes."

"So am I."

We walked to Suite 5616, Laser Computers.

"Are you the new temp?"

"Yes," I said. "Is that a problem?"

"Not at all." He smiled. "I'm your boss. Is that a problem?"

"Not at all."

My week's assignment at Laser Computers was a blast. It was a small office with only seven employees. The boss had a large office with a couch which we used morning, noon and at 5:00 o'clock quitting time. One lunch hour he had an outside appointment, but the fellow who did data entry filled in so to speak. We never told the boss and in fact, for the rest of the week, I enjoyed a 2:00 o'clock fuck in the mail room.

When that job finished I took a week off to rest my tired pussy. Every night, I had a hot bath and reminisced about those fulfilling days at Laser Computers.

18: The Virgin

After a week's rest, I was itching for a hard and fast fuck. Sometimes I liked the foreplay and the anticipation, but today I just wanted a ripe penis in and out.

I hit the mall again and went straight to the Music Store. Sam was out and there was a new fellow at the cash. When I came in, the other regular clerk whispered to the new fellow who then came over to me.

"I'm Sam's brother, Jerry, and I hear you like to look for CD's in our storeroom?"

So my reputation had preceded me. That was okay. Today I needed a quick one. "Yes, will you take me to see if we can find it?"

"Absolutely. Come this way," he said.

I smothered a laugh, thinking of how many ways I had come.

When we slipped into the narrow space, I took his hand and put it under my skirt. When he felt my bare skin, his hand dropped like a hot potato, and his eyebrows shot up like arrows. He froze and I had to unzip him and pull it out.

He was already hard and the minute I touched the tip of his penis, he came in a gush. His eyes were wide and his hands hung down at his sides shaking.

Good God! Was this his first time. "How old are you?" I said.

"Eighteen." His voice rose a pitch.

Good God. Was that legal age? "Have you done this before?"

"Nu . . . Nu . . . No."

"Why ever not?"

"I wanted to but my religion forbade it."

"I'm glad I'm not that religion." I held his limp penis in my hand. "Don't you know that God wants us to love one other?"

"But this is sex, not love."

I gently squeezed his penis and stroked along the shaft. Up and down. "Right now, I love you."

He started to get hard and I said, "Let's try again, shall we?"

"Okay," he squeaked. "What do I do?"

"Just relax and enjoy yourself. Where do you want to touch me?"

"All over."

"That's a little difficult here, but undo my blouse."

He fumbled with my buttons, finally managing to open them. My blouse hung loose.

"Now undo my bra. It fastens at the front."

He unhooked it and my breasts swelled away from their confines. He gasped.

"Now touch them. Rub them, kiss them. Do whatever you want." I rubbed his penis harder and harder as he plastered a hand on each breast. Then he squeezed in and out, a rapturous look on his face.

"Oh, blessed Mary. This feels good."

"Yes, it does."

He bent down and put his mouth over a nipple, chewing on it.

"You are a fast learner. That feels good, but go easy with the chomping." Virginia was getting wet and his cock was hard and ready. I plunged it in to me and this time he moved with me as we rocked back and forth. He buried his face between my breasts, licking and sucking them. Faster and faster we moved, coming together just as a customer poked his head through the doorway.

"Do you need any help in there?"

"We're done, thank you," I said.

"Are you sure," he goggled at my large breasts only half covered by Jerry's grasping hands.

"Another time," I said. "Now git."

The customer left and Jerry and I tidied our clothes.

"Thank you, Ma'am. Thank you so much. Thank you. That was lovely."

"See that you do more of it. It's good for you."

"Oh, I will, I will."

As I left the store and the mall, I reasoned. Well, it was fast and what the hell. Someone has to teach them.

19: Policemen to the Rescue

I was getting bolder and taking more chances. What would happen if I were caught? Is there a law about sex in public? Especially at my age. Probably. People were so uptight about sex. As if it were something bad. It would only be bad if you were non-consenting. Any man who forced himself on an unwilling woman was sick. And that wasn't about sex anyway. It was about total insecurity.

I had done it with young men, old men, fat men, skinny men, married men, single men. As long as it had a penis and was over eighteen I would do it. At least, I hoped eighteen was the legal age. I didn't want to go to jail for such a delicious pastime. I wanted to be turned on, not turned in. But it would be titillating, so to speak, to do it with a policeman.

Lots of cops were good looking and it was nice to do it with a good looking man. Maybe I could call a policeman to my home. But they usually came in twos.

Well that would be all right. But risky. Could I be so lucky as to attract two of them who would be willing and not blow the whistle on me? After all, it's probably frowned on for policemen to indulge while on duty.

That night I phoned the police station, saying I suspected someone had been following me and I feared a break in.

As I waited, I hoped the officers would be men. I was lucky—they were. From the lobby camera, I could see that one was younger, early twenties and the other looked around thirty-five. Either one would do. I buzzed them in and in a moment they were at my door. I wore a robe over my pale pink flimsy nighty—the one with the low V at the neck.

They looked around the living room and kitchen. "Everything seems okay," the older one said.

"Have you locked all your windows?" said the younger.

"I think so, but there's one in my bedroom that's hard to lock. Perhaps you could help me with that?"

"Sure." He followed me along the hall while the other one walked to the patio door leading to the balcony.

As we walked into the bedroom, the belt of my robe got "accidentally" caught on the door knob pulling my robe open. I let the belt fall to the floor and followed the officer to the window.

He easily clicked the latch.

"There you go." He turned around, startled to see me standing so close. My robe hung open showing the whole front of my see-through nighty. My breasts were less than a foot from his badge.

"Thank you so much, officer. I feel much safer now."

"Er—yes. Are there any other windows you need checking?" His gaze seemed stuck on my chest area.

"Well, there's one in the bathroom that sticks sometime."

"Show me where that is." He continued to gape at my front.

"Come with me." I led him to the bathroom.

Once in the bathroom, I shut the door. "It's so small in here. More room, with the door shut."

"Where's the window?"

"Oh, silly me. I was sure there was a window in here." We were standing close and he looked down at my breasts pushing against the thin fabric. Then he looked lower. I was not wearing underpants. His Adam's apple bobbed.

It was now or never. I took his hand and put it on my breast. He gasped, but did not remove his hand. "Do you ever help damsels in distress?" I asked.

"Are you in distress?" His voice cracked.

"Oh, yes. Great distress." I wriggled my body into his hand and stepped even closer. Then I took his other hand and cupped it between my legs. "Great distress," I repeated. "Can you do something about it?" I wiggled against his lower hand and he groaned.

I fumbled with the fly on his uniform. My god. I was going to do it with a policeman. My body trembled with excitement. I tugged at his zipper but it wouldn't move. He let go of my breast and yanked at his belt buckle, unzipped his pants and dropped them.. His penis shot through the flap in his boxers.

I scrambled to lift my nighty, and just as I got it up he plunged into me. He lifted me off my feet and banged against me. My breasts rubbed against his badge. I clung to him around the neck, letting my body do its thing. Higher and higher, high as the sky and beyond. He came and I came again and again.

I was in a daze when he hoisted his pants and carried me into the bedroom. He placed me on the bed and pulled the quilt over me.

"Is everything all right in there?"

It was the other policeman. "I've checked everything and it all seems tight."

"Everything is fine in here," the young stud said. "Nice and tight." He walked out of the bedroom, leaving the door open.

"Is the woman all right?" I heard the other fellow say.

"Oh, yes. She wanted me to see her safely in bed."

The older officer peered around the door.

I lay with the covers to my neck, my eyes closed and a smile on my face.

"Is she asleep?"

"I think so. She just crashed, after my investigation."

20: The Art of Fucking

My next temp job was to model at the Art College. No, not nude, although I would have been up for that. It was for a portrait study, so I kept all my clothes on. It was fun as I sat there and eyed the artists looking at me. There were a couple of young guys that I passed the time imagining what they could do for me.

After class and the students had left, the instructor asked if I would like to see his etchings. I nearly laughed in his face. That old line?

His studio was around the corner and I was surprised to find he actually did have etchings. Every one of them was of nude women.

"You do nudes very well," I said. "Do you use live models?"

"Oh, yes. It's the only way."

Neither of us said anything, So I did. "Could I model for you sometime?"

"Funny you should say that. I was going to ask you if you would."

"Should I show you first, to see if I am suitable."

"Good idea," he said. He sat on a chair while I undressed in front of him.

I had never done a striptease in front of a fully clothed man while he watched. Virginia got excited just at the thought.

I slipped out of my shoes and took off my blouse. I folded it neatly and put it on a chair beside his easel. I pulled my skirt down and laid if over my blouse. Down came my panty hose, added to the pile.

He sat opposite, arms folded. A scholarly look on his face. I undid my bra and let loose the girls. They liked men to look at them and fondle them. I put the bra on the chair. I slid my underpants down and added them. Naked as a jaybird, I stood and waited.

He nodded pensively. "Will you turn around, please?"

I turned around and stood with my back to him. He has to be gay. I turned back to face him.

"Are your breasts real?"

"What?" He's got to be kidding.

"I do like authenticity in my art."

I cupped my hands under the girls, lifting them proudly "100% the real thing. Come and feel if you want."

He got out of his chair with an unmistakable bulge in his pants. He put his hands on my breasts and had a really good feel.

I was getting hotter and hotter, and hoped he was going to make his next move. I was sure he wanted to.

He stepped back."I know it's a cliche for the artist to seduce his models, but do you mind?"

Finally. "It would be my pleasure. Where do you want me?"

He was pulling his pants of as he said, "The couch would be ideal. That's where all my models pose."

By the time I stepped to the couch and lay down, he was on top of me, nude from the waist down.

He didn't waste any time. I was wet and ready and he plunged in. And out and in satisfying both of us greatly.

Afterward, I lay there while he took a pad of paper and a pencil and rapidly made some sketches. It felt nice being looked at while he did it. I wondered what it would be like to lay naked in front of the whole class.

I found out the next day. When I turned up for his art class he announced to the class this was to be a figure drawing and that Ms. Somerville would be happy to oblige.

There was a curtained off area at the side of the room, where I took off my clothes. I actually felt nervous, but I must admit excited about walking out in front of twenty-five students—about half of them male.

"Where do you want me?" I could have bitten my tongue. What a dumn thing to say.

There were titters from the class.

He indicated a padded chaise lounge. "There would be fine. Just make yourself comfortable."

I stretched out on my side, with my front showing to the class. The students picked up their pencils and with glances back and forth from me to their papers they scribbled away for twenty slow minutes. It's hard work doing nothing. I amused myself by staring at each man, trying to catch their eye, but they were looking at my body parts. How can they not get aroused?

"Time," the instructor said.

Glad to move, I stretched my arms over my head and wriggle around getting the kinks out. Several of the men were still looking at me, their pencils held aloft. I suspected that was not the only thing that was aloft.

After an hour, I was exhausted and thankful the class was over. But I was so aroused I desperately needed a fuck.

The students packed up their supplies and were leaving. I went behind the curtain to get dressed, but I hesitated. *Please one of you guys come around here. I need some instant service.*

The art teacher called out. "Ms Somerville, would you mind waiting one moment before you get dressed?"

I poked my head around the curtain. Not at all.

A handsome young man was standing beside the teacher. "I am studying human mating rituals and I wonder if you could help me out?"

My heart beat faster. "I will if I can. What do you want me to do."

"Well, I'd like to sketch a man and a woman in various mating positions. Of course, you don't have to actually mate, but just pretend to."

Another student stepped out from behind him.

His bulge said he was ready. Pretend or not.

"I've never done anything like that before, but I'm willing to try. For the sake of art."

The second young man ripped off his clothes and flung them on a chair. "Ready." His cock stood up high.

The artist said, "Show me missionary position first."

I went back to the posing couch, lay down and the hot guy came over and lay on top of me. His penis looking for a place to land.

"It looks like the only place to put that is inside me," I said.

"Are you sure you don't mind?" His voice shook.

"Not at all."

He quickly found the place and glided it in. We fucked merrily on the couch in front of the artist and the teacher.

When we were finished, they thanked us very much for actually doing it. "I got some really good sketches," said the student. "Could I trouble you to show me a doggie position now?"

I wasn't sure I could handle another real fuck. "I will have to pretend on that one. I'm all fucked out."

The student who had done his duty so well, was limp and exhausted. "I don't think I could even pretend. I can hardly stand."

"No problem," the teacher said. "I could stand in, so to speak."

He whipped all his clothes off while I turned over and lay on my stomach.

He kneeled over me and lifted me up on my hands and knees. His stiff cock brushed against my bum. I tilted my behind up so he could reach Virginia who was willing again. That girl never ceased to amaze me.

He didn't stick it in right away. His hands reached under me and played with my dangling breasts, making my thighs tingle. Then his prick found the opening and dove right in. It was another fine fuck, made ever more delightful to have an audience of two other men.

After that, they called out for pizza and sodas and we sat around nude eating and drinking. By now, the mating artist was nude too and when we had polished off the pizza he politely asked if I would mind if he took a turn.

"Why not? It's for art."

He was a lovely fuck as well. I couldn't help seeing, out of the corner of my eye, that while we were fully engaged in human mating, the other two were having some fun with each other as well.

Thank you, God, for inventing sex.

21: A Police Encore

I took another day off from work and from fucking. A girl can only take so much pleasure.

However, I was getting another hankering for police service sand when I called the police station I was lucky to get my same two guys. I was ready for them with same robe over the same see-through nighty.

They walked in. "What seems to be the trouble?" The older one said very professionally.

"I just don't understand it. I can't seem to tighten the locks on my windows."

"They can be finicky," the young one said. "How is that one in your bathroom doing?"

"Oh, that one's okay, but now the bedroom window needs some attention. Shall I show you where it is—in case you've forgotten?"

"I have a pretty good memory, but why don't you."

We walked into the bedroom and he closed the door. He put his hand on his belt buckle and waiting. I undid the sash of my robe, but before I could take it off, he had dropped his pants and was fumbling with my nighty. I helped him lift it and his probing penis found its way to where we both wanted it. Holding me to him, we hobbled to the bed and fell on top.

We bounced madly on my quilt and with that sweet policeman in me, I came again and again to heights of ecstasy. He rolled over, breathing hard. After a moment, he got up and pulled his pants up, zipped, and buckled his belt.

"How is the damsel now?"

"I'm just great," I murmured from a faraway place.

"I'll check how my partner's doing. And we'll be going."

"Hmmm. I'm fine now."

It was about an hour later when my buzzer sounded again. I had just made a pot of camomile to luxuriate in my recent sexual encounter. Sometimes, reliving it was almost as good as the real thing. I had a wonderful imagination.

Peering through the peep hole I saw that it was a policeman, his head averted. Had he come back for more? Well, I guess I would be up for it, although it was a little soon. I would have been fine for another day. I opened the door and was surprised to see not the young officer, but his partner.

"Good evening, ma'am."

"Good evening."

He removed his hat. "I was just going off duty, and I wanted to check if everything was still all right here."

"Come in." Did he know? Should I risk it with him too?

I had changed my nighty into my royal blue see-through one. I only owned see-throughs. My same robe, loosely tied, covered it. "I just made a cup of tea. Would you like one?"

"That would be mighty fine." He followed me to the kitchen.

"How long have you been partners with the other officer?"

"Going on three years now. We're good friends. We share everything."

"Oh, really?"

He had that look in his eyes. He knew. Should I play a little with him, or just get to it? "What kind of things do you share?"

"Oh, you know. Baseball, donuts—pretty well everything."

I poured the tea and carried the mugs to the living room. He followed closely—very closely— behind. When I got to the coffee table, I stopped suddenly and he bumped against me. I could feel the rising lump in his pants. I stood. Waiting.

He slid his hands around the front of me and undid my sash. It fell to the rug and my robe opened. Then his hands moved to my breasts, cupping them. I still held a hot mug of tea in each hand as he pressed his body against my bottom and massaged my breasts.

My crotch tingled. I wanted him in me and all over me.

"Let me put the tea down," I said, and bent over and put the cups on the coffee table. When I straightened up, he pulled the robe off my shoulders, removed it and tossed it at the couch. I heard a buckle open and his zipper go down.

"Bend over again," he whispered in my ear.

Did he want to feel my dangling breasts? Some men liked that. I bent over and immediately felt my nightly being pulled up over my bum. Strong hands grasped the sides of my hips and lifted me. Then a stiff penis, probing for its place. He was doing it doggy fashion. I bent way over to make it easier and he plunged into Virginia. His hands were on my breasts, as he banged back and forth.

This was the second I had been fucked from behind and I liked it. It felt so animalistic. I fell into the rhythm, as he fucked his and my brains out. He finished with a shout and grabbed me from falling. I was practically unconscious. He turned me over, picked me up and placed me on the couch. The tea was still hot.

"How are you now, my damsel in distress?"

I couldn't speak for a moment. Two policemen in one night. "I am filled to the brim."

"We serve to please," he said. "I hate to run but I have to go."

"Hmmmm."

"Perhaps me and my partner should check you out next week."

"Hmmm." I was dozy, my body still tingling.

"Just to be sure you're okay here, living all alone."

"Hmmmm." I was still in bliss.

"Would that be okay?"

"Absolutely officer. You can both come again and take care of me."

He left quietly and I fell asleep with a big smile.

22: Even More Policemen

The next night I was watching a rerun of Sex in the City. It had been a slow day at the office. No sex but a couple of maybe's for the next day. I had just had a perfumed bath and was dressed in my usual see-through nighty, contemplating pleasuring myself when my buzzer sounded.

I peered through the eye hole. Two policemen, but not the ones from last night. I opened the door.

"Hello, ma'am. We had a report that there was a damsel in distress. Would that be you?"

"Well, well," I said, assessing the situation. Usually, I had to find the men. Now they were finding me. "Perhaps. How do you help damsels in distress?"

"Whatever is needed," the big one said. He took a step toward me. "What do you need?" He looked at my see-through nighty under my half-tied robe.

Did he see my nipples rising?

"We work as a team," the other policeman said.

"A team? What does that mean?"

"We do it together."

Had my wildest fantasy come true? Two men at once. "Do come in." Excitement started to churn in my inner recesses as I thought of those two good looking uniformed men crawling all over me at the same time.

They entered and shut the door. "We heard you like policemen."

"Well, the two I've met have certainly been fulfilling."

"We'd like to show you just what we can offer," the big one said, and with that he undid his buckle and dropped his pants. His penis jumped out.

"You don't waste any time, do you."

"No ma'am. We liked to get the job done, and no time like the present and I have a big present. for you."

He took a step toward me and opened my robe.

My body leapt to life while my mind gambolled after it to catch up.

He knelt down and stuck his head under my nightly and lapped and probed with his tongue. I squirmed with pleasure, pushing my hips forward to get more of him. I looked over his head to see the other cop open his fly and bring out an oversized cock which he jerked back and forth vigorously.

I wanted one of those cocks in me and just as I thought that, the guy under my nighty lifted his dripping face and pulled me to the floor.

Then he lay over me and shoved his cock into me all the way. I could hardly breath he was so big but I hung in as he bounced up and down. He finished with a shout, pulled out and rolled off me.

The other guy dropped his rock hard cock and kneeled over me. "Want some of this?"

I hadn't come and needed him. "Bring it on," I said. "I can take it." But looking at the size of him, I began to wonder if I could.

He touched the tip of his huge penis at the opening of Virginia and pushed it in about an inch. I was still plenty wet and that felt nice.He pushed it in further. I could feel my insides stretching to accommodate his thick shaft. On he went. Further and further, until I thought he would come out the other side. He touched places I didn't even know I had, and I pumped against him with renewed vigour. I felt like a virgin all over again. He was even bigger than the Janitor.

"Don't stop," I yelled. "Don't ever stop."

"Don't worry," he grunted. "I won't." He held my buttocks in his big hands and ground me until I thought I would split in two. The room began to spin and I felt myself getting larger than life. Then everything went black.

The next thing I knew I was on top of my bed, totally naked.

The two cops were standing at the end of the bed. They were naked too and both of them had a hard on. These guys must take their vitamins.

"What happened?" I said.

"You kinda fainted," the big one said. "Sorry about that. I have that effect on the ladies."

"It was worth it."

"Have you had enough or would you like some more?"

Such gentlemen, these cops. I wasn't sure if I wanted more right then, but what an opportunity. Two strong men ready and willing to do whatever I wanted.

"I am a little tired, but what more can you do?"

They looked at each other. Smiled and each walked up a side of the bed. "You just lay there ma'am and we'll service you."

One of them straddled me, bent over and sucked one hard nipple and then the other. As he was doing this, he gently slipped his cock inside me and moved back and forth in an easy rhythm. Meanwhile the other fellow came to the head of the bed and climbed on my face.

His penis had nowhere to go but into my mouth, so I sucked him while the other one fucked me. Then they changed places and I sucked the other guy while he fucked me. I was so far out of it, I started to enjoy sucking them.

I wanted it to last forever, but as they say, all good things must come to an end. All three of us came at the same time, warm semen filling my mouth and Ginny. Filling and overflowing. Warm and milky and dripping over me. I felt as if I had been christened. My heart beat fast and my body shot electric spikes from every pore.

We lay exhausted for several minutes. Finally the cops stood up.

"You guys are a great team," I said.

"We do our best."

I was exhausted and filled to the brim.

They pulled on their pants, shirts and jackets. As they stood at the bedroom door, the big one said, "Now don't you hesitate to call if you're in need of anything at anytime. Just call the precinct and ask for Ned or Jim and we'll be at your disposal."

"I'll do that," I said and closed my eyes. I needed to rest my aching and quivering body.

I heard the door shut and I lay there for several minutes, replaying the fantastic antics. After what must have been ten minuted I heard the door open. Had they forgotten something?

"Whose there?" I called.

"No worry, ma'am. We're policemen."

Three uniformed policemen walked into my bedroom and stood in a row at the bottom of my bed. What was going on? I didn't even have the presence of mind to cover myself. The three of them just stood there and stared at my bare breasts and my spread apart legs.

"What do you want?" I said.

"What do you think?" one of them said.

I stared back. This was impossible. Was I up for this? I was still in the aftermath of the other two and my whole body felt sexed out. "Maybe another day, guys. I'm a little tired right now."

"But we're here now and I'm sure you don't want to disappoint us. We hear you like policemen."

"I do, but—"

"Tell you what ma'am. Why don't we just undress and let you decide? We won't force you to do anything, but if you see something you like here, you just let us know."

With that, they took off their clothes. I lay back and watched as shoes, socks, buckles, pants, jackets, shirts, and shorts were discarded and placed on chairs and in a pile on the floor.

Three well built naked men stood before me, penises growing steadily higher until all three stood up.

This was a test. I said I liked sex. Here was my chance to really have a go at it and with three fine specimens. Somewhere I got my second wind and my body rose to the occasion.

"You," I said and pointed to the first one.

"Yes, ma'am. What can I do for you?"

"I'm sure you'll think of something." He stepped toward me. I pointed to the next one. "You too." He came over. "And you," I said to the final one.

Three naked male bodies descended on me. One licked my clitoris, one stuck his penis in my mouth. The other squeezed my breasts around his rigid rod as he rubbed it back and forth. My whole body was singing, and stinging, overloaded with joy.

They moved from place to place on me. I shut my eyes and let whatever happen happen. Strong hands, male mouths, hard cocks, in me, over me around me, through me. I was in surrender heaven. Just laying there and letting them play with me felt so freeing. I didn't have to decide what I wanted. Let them do their thing on me, to me, and with me. I knew they wouldn't hurt me, so I gave in completely.

One of them lifted me to my hands and knees and entered me from behind, holding my breasts and slapping my bum lightly. As soon as he came, the other one turned me over and pushed his penis in at the front, pushing and banging on me until he came, to be replaced instantly with another hard cock. An assembly line of sex. I came over and over and over. My rockets sending me over the edge. to paradise and beyond.

They must have been taking some drug to have them become erect again, because doing round robin they must have entered me and come at least three times each. But who was counting. I was in sexual bliss. Virginia was starting to go numb, if that was possible. I thought she would never tire.

After the never ending round of having things shoved up me: fingers, cocks, and tongues, they finally rolled off the bed. I lay there like a rag doll and watched them get dressed.

"Thank you ma'am. That was mighty nice," the first one said.

"You are some fucking woman," the second one said.

"You get the medal for endurance," the third one said.

I couldn't speak. I was in a stupor. Semen covered me. Over me, in my hair, in my bedclothes. Virginia throbbed. Definitely sexual overload.

"Lock the door when you go out," I called after then.

I heard the door click shut and I fell into a dreamless sleep.

23: One for the Rookie

The next morning I could hardly move. My body hurt all over. Muscles I didn't know I had ached and my vagina felt like it had been stampeded by a hundred horses.

I stumbled to the bathroom and turned on the taps for a long hot bath. I soaked for over an hour, adding hot water as the water cooled.

After a whole pot of camomile tea, I tackled the bedclothes and threw them all into the washer. My nightly lay torn on the living room floor and I threw that out.

I put on a long terry towel robe, curled up in my favourite chair with another cup of tea and relived the night before. I could hardly believe that five policemen had fucked me—all in the same night. In two and threes no less.

That was a first. Maybe I will write a book. Maybe other people would like to hear that sexual fantasies do come true.

I was in no shape to go to work so I phoned in and told the agency I was going on a week's holiday. I needed a rest from sex—I didn't tell her that—and I didn't even masturbate. I had had enough to last me for a good while.

Late that afternoon, a sole policeman knocked on my door. He looked like a rookie and said that Joe sent him.

"What for?" I opened the door a crack, keeping the chain lock on.

"You know, for—" His face reddened.

"I don't know what you're talking about young man? For what?"

"They said you liked policemen to—you know. Do things to you."

"Do things? What kind of things? The poor kid. But I couldn't help it.

"Well, er—"

There I was in my sweats, no bra and my hair in a ponytail. I must have looked like an ordinary bored housewife. Certainly not a sex object like he must have been told. I spoke sharply. "What is it young man? What do you want?'

"Sorry, ma'am. I must have the wrong address." He turned to go.

I felt so sorry for him. "Just a minute." I pulled the chain off and opened the door. "Come in for one minute. Maybe I can think of something to show you."

He looked confused, but walked in. I shut the door behind him. "Did you mean something like this?"

I lifted my shirt and he stared at my large breasts.

"Would you like to touch them?"

His eyes got bigger and he lifted two shaking hands.

'That feels good," I said, "And it wold be nice if you suck them."

He gasped and stuck his head up my shirt fastening his mouth on one nipple and his hand busy massaging the other one. It felt really good to be felt up like that and I could tell he was having a really good time. I couldn't believe it, but my crotch started to tingle. Well, let it tingle. Nothing is getting in there for at least a week.

"How are you doing?" I called.

He popped his head out with a big grin. "You have amazing tits. They are so soft and big." Both his hands were still busy, kneading them like dough.

The bulge in his pants had grown somewhat. I wasn't big on blow jobs, but he was so sweet and Virginia was too worn out to oblige him.

"How would you like to do a sixty-nine"

His eyes bulged as big as his pants were getting. "You mean—."

"Let's go to the couch. It's cozy there. But be gentle. Just tongue. No fingers and definitely no cock in my ginny. Agreed?"

"Absolutely." He cried, and ran to the couch. He lay down and undid his zipper. His shaft shot out.

"Well, you are ready," I said.

I pulled my sweats and underpants down to my thighs and lay down on top of him with my cunt in his face. He grabbed my behind, pulled it to him, and stuck his tongue in lapping and sucking. I held his stiff rod in both hands and put my lips around the tip.

I played with it for a bit nibbling and sucking and then slowly slid it in and out of my mouth. He groaned and wriggled and bounced and came in a whoosh. What the hell. I heard it was good for the complexion so I swallowed the whole thing.

I had a good time. Just a regular orgasm but that was okay. I could do a good deed now and then. Men had been so generous to me.

I rolled off him and pulled my pants up. He lay there like a puppy, still panting.

"How was that?" I asked.

He grinned like the cheshire cat, as he did up his zipper and stood up.

At the door, he turned. "You are amazing. Can I come again?"

"That would be nice. You come so beautifully. However, I am taking a week off. I'll let the precinct know when I'm ready for another visit."

"I'll tell the fellows. We'll take good care of you."

"Oh, I'm sure you will. Bye bye."

I leaned against the closed the door. Life was so great. I had a a whole stable of studs ready to service me.

Thank god for men and their beautiful penises, for their sticks, their rods, their cocks, their Peters, and Charles Sr.

Their soldiers and pricks. Call them what you like as long as they were shoved into me to bring me to the heights of pleasure. I was grateful that I knew who to call whenever I needed a sex fix.

Heaven.

24: Holy Sex

After my week's rest, I went back to work. The precinct called to see if I needed anything and I let them know I needed a further break. They were understanding when I promised them a visit soon. I couldn't believe it, but I was wanting something new and different.

What about a priest? That would be a real high. Were they all gay? Somehow I doubted it. They must have a struggle with sex, being men. But where would I find a priest? Well, a church of course. I went to several Catholic churches until I found a good looking young priest. I could tell he wasn't gay, because when I stood beside him, I could feel the heat coming from him, right through his cassock.

One Sunday, I stayed after the service and asked if I could speak to him about a delicate matter.

"Of course, my child, what is it."

I lowered my eyes. "Well, I'm embarrassed to talk about it, especially to a priest."

"You do not have to be embarrassed."

"It's about sex"

"Oh, I see. Is there someone else you can talk to? Perhaps a therapist, or a woman friend?"

"Oh, no. This is too embarrassing."

"Well, I don't know if I can help."

"My problem is that I am afraid that I might be attracted to women. I am shy with men and I don't know if I could respond to one."

"Well, one must be married before indulging in sex."

"But time is marching on and I don't know if I'll ever find a husband and if I do what if I disappoint him. What if I'm a lesbian. Shouldn't I find out before I get married?"

"Same sex is a sin, my child."

"I know. That's why I'm afraid of it. I really want to be attracted to a man but—"

" I don't see how I can help."

"You're a man, Father."

"I am a priest."

"Of course you are and that's why it's so perfect. I can see if I am attracted to you and I will be safe with you because you won't do anything."

"It is out of the question."

"But father, I will kill myself unless I know if I am attracted to men. Please help me."

"Suicide is also a sin."

"Please Father. You can help me not be a lesbian or not kill myself. All I need is to know if I am attracted to you."

"Well —what would I have to do."

"We would have to go somewhere private. Other people wouldn't understand."

We walked back to the robing room. There was a small desk and stalls with robes hanging. "We will be private here," he said.

"I need you to touch me to see if I like it or not."

"What do you mean touch you? Hold your hand?"

"That would be a start."

He took my hand.

"That feels nice," I said. "But I still don't feel any desire for you."

"This is very awkward."

His hand trembled in mine.

"Oh, I so do appreciate you doing this. I know I am putting you out and that you feel nothing for women. That is why you are so perfect. Don't make me kill myself."

The priest's face went white.

I opened my blouse. A lacy brassiere poked out through my shirt. I took his hand and placed it over a breast

He stiffened but did not draw his hand away.

I moved his hand back and forth. "Nothing yet," I said, but my nipple tingled. "I need you to feel my skin." I snapped my bra open from the front, freeing its soft mounds.

A strangled cry came from the priest.

I moved his hand over my bare breast and wriggled into it. "Oh, I think I'm feeling something. Yes, that does feel nice."

'Okay, we're finished." He pulled his hand from the hot fire.

"But I'm not sure what I'm feeling," I said. I put his hand on my breast again. He didn't stop me. His robe stirred as life rose beneath it.

"Oh, thank you, father, for letting your body respond. That will help me so much."

The priest gasped and rubbed my breast harder.

I undid the zipper of my skirt and let it fall. I wore only a thong which I undid with a side clasp. It fell to the ground leaving my bottom naked.

"Oh," the priest croaked. "Oh, my."

I took one of his hands and placed it between my legs. His index finger slipped inside me and he groaned, leaning on my shoulder.

"That feels very good, father, I think I do like men."

His finger kept moving and I got wetter. I lifted his robes and found his throbbing penis. Guiding it to where his hand was I planted myself on top of it.

"Arrrgg," he cried and began pumping in and out.

"Oh, yes, Father this is good. I do like it. I do. Keep doing that."

He didn't stop. He put his mouth on my breast and his hands cupped my bare bottom as he pulled me to him again and again. With a cry he exploded inside me and I rode the roller coaster to heaven.

He pulled away and fell on his knees crying, "What have I done? What have I done?"

I knelt in front of him. "It's all right Father. You have saved me. God will surely forgive you for that."

My breasts pushed past my open bra, my womanhood showing between my open knees. His gaze wandered from my breasts to my crotch. His member rose and I said, "Oh, Father, please do it again. That will surely convince me I am not a lesbian."

We rolled to the floor and he stuck his rock hard penis into me. I pushed myself up and down. "Oh, yes. Father. This feels good. I'm pretty sure now that I'm attracted to men. Thank you so much for helping me." I continued to purr and push and slide back and forth. He panted and made strangling noises as he came in a rush. My breast lay against his cassock and he pulled his robe open and tore it off. Then his undergarments. I removed my blouse and bra. We lay together naked.

"Like Adam and Eve," I said with a smile.

I bent down and kissed the tip of his wet penis and he went ballistic. He started feeling me all over. He stuck his fingers in every orifice. In my mouth, in my ass, in my wet and dripping vagina. He put his mouth on each breast, sucking and licking. He knelt down and licked between my legs. I wriggled and jiggled and his penis grew big again.

"Father, you surprise me. I picked the right person to help me with my problem. Thank you so much."

"You're welcome, my child," he said, and plunged into me for the third time.

He had a nice body, strong and responsive. It renewed my faith in men to have sex this way. They didn't all do it with their pants on.

There was a knock on the door.

"Are you in there, Father." It was his housekeeper.

At that moment, he was deep inside me.

"I am in, but I'm busy right now," he managed to say.

"Are you all right. It sounds as if you are laboring at something."

"It's nothing I can't manage," he said with another thrust.

"Let me know when you're all done," she said.

" It won't be long now."

I would have laughed if I wasn't intent on coming myself. The hardy priest was bringing me to the rapture point again and he burst inside me just as I sailed through a ceiling of delight.

We lay wrapped in each others arms, he still inside me. It felt so good.

After a long while, we unwound, and got dressed. He watched me put on my thong and bra, having one more kiss on each breast before I covered up. The thong did not cover my backside curves and he had another caress and lick before I put my skirt on.

"Thank you Father. I am sure now that I'm attracted to men. Thank you so much."

"But what now?"

"What do you mean?"

"I cannot be a priest after this."

"Why not? It was done with the purist of reasons. I'm sure your bishop would understand."

"It's not that. I want to do this again. Lots of times and only with you."

"Oh, my."

"Is that a problem?"

"I guess not. I could come by now and then. I like it that you're a priest."

"Then I will stay a priest for you and for the cause. I wouldn't want you to kill yourself or become a lesbian."

"You are so kind. It will be our secret."

So that took care of Sundays. I looked forward to my weekly visit with the priest. I tried to keep it fresh so we did it in various parts of the church. Once we did it when the housekeeper was in the next room. She called through the door that he shouldn't work so hard.

Another time, we tried it on a pew but that was way too uncomfortable—too narrow and too hard—so we usually kept to his private rooms.

A few times I went early to the church service and sat where he could see me. I'd lick my lips and smile and he would stutter and stammer. Then when we got together after, he would be mad for me.

One day, I had to sit at the back. The church was crowded and the sermon long. I was getting bored and Virginia was longing for the priest's gentle touch. The man to the right of me seemed bored too so I thought I would have some extra curricular fun. First I casually draped my scarf over my lap. Then I reached to my right, took his hand which was resting on his knee, and placed it under my scarf.

He glanced over, but I looked straight ahead as if nothing was happening. After a moment, and as my lover priest droned on, I guided the man's fingers through my side zipper and into my pants. I just had to start him and he continued the exploring. He wasn't bored any longer. I saw his bulge pressing out and was sorry I couldn't do anything for him right then, but he seemed to enjoy it when his fingers found their way between my legs. Virginia was already wet and he wiggled his forefinger into me and shoved it in and out like a little penis. It felt so great, I wanted to shout.

But then everyone started standing up for a hymn. We rose together, his finger still in me, and I held the scarf over my front. I could hardly breath, it felt so good. I had to hold myself back from panting and yelling. The song ended, and people knelt. OMG. He had added another finger and the two together felt more like a penis. I reached over and put my hand over his bulge and pressed. He undid his zipper and slid my hand onto his cock. My scarf was big enough to cover us both and I rubbed him back and forth as he continued to finger fuck me. He pulled out a handkerchief and stuffed it into his fly as he came and I wished I had one. I was sopping wet and when he finally pulled his fingers out of me, I was weak and totally satisfied.

When the congregation filed out, it was crowded and our row waited for the aisle to clear. The man behind me was standing very close and I felt something touching my bum. A hand clasped it and another one slid down my waistband and over my bare skin. Good heavens the man on my left must have known what had happened. I was so intent I didn't even notice who had been sitting on the other side of me. I pressed my back to him and this allowed his hand to reach down between my legs. I was still wet and his fingers easily slid in the opening. These church going men knew a good thing when they saw it.

I tilted my pelvis so he could go in further and as we stood waiting for people to leave, I totally enjoyed that anonymous set of fingers having a good time with me.

As the crowd thinned and our row started moving, he gave a last thrust and pulled his hand out of my pants. I didn't look back as my two finger-fuckers went out and I made my way through the crowd to the front of the church.

The visit that afternoon with the priest was especially fun as I relived my interlude with the sexually talented parishioners. As the priest pumped away on me, I received his blessing with gratitude. Life was so good. God is in heaven and all was well with the world.

25: The Doctor Is In

I thought it would be a fine experience to do it with a doctor. So many doctors are stuffy and always in a rush. It was magical how I picked the one who would respond. He was East Indian, very handsome and very proper. I pretended that I had a pain in my stomach and the nurse told me to wait in a small room, one of three in a row. I stripped all my clothes off and put on the paper coat, open down the front.

When the doctor came in, I was sitting on the edge of a high cushioned gurney thing. "You didn't need to take off all your clothes," he said.

"Oh, silly me. I thought I did."

"And you have the gown on backwards."

"I wondered about that. But I guess the human body is nothing to you, Doctor." I let the paper gown fall open.

"Well, let's see what we have here."

He pushed warm brown fingers against my stomach and, looking up in the air, said, "Does that hurt."

"No,"

He moved his fingers to the side. "What about that?"

"That tickles."

"And this?" His hand went lower. The tingle started.

"A little," I lied.

He moved his hand lower. Getting close to my inner sanctum.

I breathed out. "That feels good."

He took his hand away and looked at me with a penetrating gaze.

I said, "I'm not sure now. Perhaps you should do that again."

His dark eyes bore into me. Did he know what I wanted? Would he do it? He could lose his license. He turned away and I said, "I think I have women's problems. I would really like you to investigate."

"I'll get my glove."

"Is that necessary?"

"Lie back," he said.

I lay down and placed my legs on the stirrups. It felt nice having my legs splayed apart with my private parts exposed and waiting.

The nurse came in and the doctor said, "Nurse, I have to do an internal. You need to stay."

"Yes, doctor."

He reached down with a gloved hand and inserted two fingers into me. I wanted to wriggle and squeal with delight but couldn't with the nurse there. He probed around. "Feels okay," he said and withdrew his hand.

I was pulsating and needed more. And not with plastic.

"Thank you Nurse, that will be all," he said.

The nurse left and as soon as the door was closed, he flicked off the glove and plunged his bare fingers into me, pleasuring Virginia greatly. I groaned and pushed into his hand. His other hand stroked my breasts, making me wild with desire. His fingers knew exactly where to touch and when and how much. He brought me to the brink and then pulled away. He kept doing this and just when I couldn't stand it, he took me over the top.

I shuddered as my body crested again and again. He pulled his wet hand out of me, dried it off and said, "I recommend you receive weekly treatments of this."

With that he left the room. I lay limp and sailed through the universal tides for a long while before I got dressed. On my way out, I made an appointment for next Thursday.

On Thursday, I didn't have sex all day, keeping myself pure for my doctor's visit. He must have made some arrangement with the nurse because once I was shown into the cubicle I never saw the nurse again. I disrobed and lay on the paper on the examining table, my legs positioned in the stirrups. I didn't bother putting on the disposable gown.

The doctor came in and locked the door behind him.

"How are we today, Ms. Somerville?"

"We are anxiously awaiting your examination."

"Do you think it's women's problems again?"

"Oh, definitely, doctor. My problem needs your special attention." He must have written, not just read, the Kama Sutra. Again his fingers knew just where and when to touch, and how to tease me into realms of anticipation that made me rise up off the table, begging him to finish me off.

"You're killing me," I wailed. "Hurry, hurry, do it, do it, now, right now." I wriggled and pushed and reached for his pants. I wanted all of him to crawl inside me and explode his sizzling fuse.

Only when I panted like a wounded beast, my face flushed and my body crying for mercy did he bring me to the fullness of my being. Skyrockets shot through every cell, every pore and every particle of my being. My soul sang arias and crashing chords of chimes, bells and gongs went off.

He took his fingers out, washed his hands and left the room. I shook for ten minutes.

The next week, no matter who I had sex with, I kept thinking of my next doctor's appointment. When the day arrived, I bathed and fussed and arrived a half hour early.

I entered the cubicle undressed, and lay naked with my feet in the stirrups and legs splayed. Waiting for my brown god.

The door opened and an English accent said, "Oh my. What have we here?"

I lifted my head and looked between my feet at a man in a white coat but not my doctor. "Who are you?"

"I am Doctor Davidson."

"But where is my regular doctor?"

"He had an emergency. What seems to be your trouble? Most women do not remove all their clothing for a pap smear."

I had better be careful. I didn't want to get my doctor in trouble. "Oh, I am a nude dancer, so being nude doesn't bother me."

He put on a glove, did his business in a very business like way and I didn't wriggle a bit.

He left, I got dressed and hoped my doctor would be available next time.

He was. I phoned ahead to be sure. The waiting room was full and one by one, people were directed to one of the three cubicles. My beautiful doctor hurried from one to the other, giving the nurse and his receptionist orders in between. He didn't look at me once and I was getting wet anticipating my time with him.

Finally, the nurse came to me. "This way, Ms. Somerville."

I followed her, but not to one of the cubicles. The nurse led me to another room further down the hall. This one had a desk, two soft armchairs—and a couch.

"Wait here, please. The doctor will be with you shortly."

I wasn't sure where to sit, so picked one of the chairs. I also didn't know if I should undress. I waited. My crotch tingled.

The doctor entered. "How are we feeling today, Ms. Somerville? Still having that women's problem?"

"Yes, indeed, doctor."

"Then let's have a look. Why don't you come over here to the couch?"

"Gladly."

I sat on the edge and he came toward me.

"Let's make you more comfortable." He bent over and took off my shoes. Then he unbuttoned my blouse and peeled it off. His hands brushed my skin.

Then he put his soft lips to my shoulder and my arm, my elbow and my wrist, kissing each spot like a delicate flower. He reached behind and unhooked my bra and slid it off. He cupped one full breast in both hands and reached down and kissed the nipple. He repeated with the other one. My crotch was on fire. Would he hurry up?

He stood up and, taking my hands, pulled me up off the couch. He undid my skirt and let it drop. Then he kneeled and lifted one of my feet and took the skirt off, then the other foot and the skirt was free. I stood naked except for my panties.

Still kneeling, he reached up and slowly peeled them over my hips and down my legs and off. His face was an inch from my steaming crotch and he kissed it slowly, his tongue poking in every so slightly. I pushed myself into his face, wanting more. Wanting all of his tongue, his fingers, his penis inside me.

But he stood up and said, "Lie down, please."

I did and he left the room. My body was humming and trembling.

He came back in a few minutes. "One of the other doctors is filling in for me. I can give you my complete attention."

He stood before me and slowly stripped off his clothes. As he removed each piece, he folded it and placed it on a chair. His brown body glowed like a sexual god and his penis stuck out like an ancient warrior's sword.

I gasped and lifted my arms up.

"Slowly, my dear. It is better done slowly."

For the next hour this incredible man, pleasured me beyond my hopes and dreams. He licked me in places I didn't know a tongue could reach. He touched and probed and stroked and kneaded my receptive skin. His penis was alive in me and before he or I came, he would pull it out and drip one drop of golden dew on my heaving stomach. Over and over, he brought me to the brink, until finally his beautiful body lay flat on top of me.

His huge penis was full inside me and it stayed there. Moving gently and slowly and then with more and more speed and vigour until it was a piston going full blast and crashing through the walls of time and space, sending me into another century, another life, another eon of raw sexuality.

I lay spent and drained and yet wholly complete, thoroughly fucked by the Indian God of Sex, disguised as an ordinary doctor.

26: The More The Merrier

I thought I had tried everything with sex. I had done it in buses, trains, planes, subways. With priests, firemen, policemen and doctors.

And then at one of my temp jobs after a quick fuck in the supply room, he invited me to a special party. He gave me the address and on Saturday night, I rang the bell.

A butler type fellow answered the door and showed me to a room where I was given a white silk robe to put on. As instructed, I stripped bare, and put on the flowing robe. I was also supplied with a white eye mask. When I went into the main room, five other people were gathered all wearing similar robes—three men wore black eye masks and black robes, the two women wore white.

The men were all handsome and the women beautiful— one with long red hair and the other had a short black pixie cut. I must have been the token older woman.

We were led into another room with tables. The idea was to sit at a table with your hands folded on top and no matter what happened, you were to show no expression. If you did, you were out of the game and had to sit on the sidelines.

Everyone had a glass of wine in front of them. I sat and took a sip. In a moment the man opposite me groaned and went glassy eyed. He left the table. What had happened to him? In the next moment, I felt someone or something under the table lift my robe.

Next, I felt something soft moving up my leg. It was not unpleasant but I wondered what it was. A velvet glove? It crawled up my thigh and reached between my legs, stopping short. I kept my face neutral, even though I wanted to shout for it to keep going. It tapped against the entrance to my vagina and I got wet. I wanted whatever it was to continue on its journey but it didn't. I took a drink and nodded to the others as if nothing was happening.

The red headed woman beside me shivered and squealed. She left the table. I slid a little forward in my seat so that whatever it was, when it came back, could easily enter me. But how could I sit still, feeling such pleasure? It came back. This time it was larger. It felt like a penis but how could it be? Perhaps it was a dildo? It had ripples on it, and was slowly pushed into me and then in and out with a steady rhythm. I wanted to holler and scream but I also didn't want it to stop so I kept my face neutral. I spread my legs wider and wriggled imperceptibly so as not to show over the table top. While this was happening, another person left the table, and then another and another.

Soon, there was only one man and myself remained. We stared at each other. By the look on his face, he was barely holding on. Which one would break first? The strokes between my legs got faster and faster and I wanted to bounce with it, but I held on, willing my face to remain calm while my lower half screamed with delight.

Just as I couldn't take another second, the man opposite shouted and slumped over. He left the table. I had won the game but the object pulled out of me before I was finished.

Everyone clapped for my win but I was agitated with frustration, feeling stuck on the top rung of a roller coaster that had skidded to a stop.

"Someone came over and lifted my hand. "The winner."

What did that mean?

"You now get to choose whoever or how many ever you want of either sex to do your bidding."

"I want a man with a big penis to finish me off," I said. They all laughed and the three men stood up. They parted their robes, and a stiff penis poked out of each one. They were all thick and throbbing, so I ran to the closest one and jumped on. I wrapped my legs around him and rode him.

The others watched, cheering and clapping. One of the men parted the robe of another woman and his penis found a ready home. The other couple masturbated each other while watching us fuck.

I came with a shout. After we parted, another man came up to me.

"Would you like to try me?" he said, withdrawing from his satisfied partner.

"Why not?"

His penis hardened again, and I climbed on. As we fucked, the two women had their hands under each other robes. One man openly masturbated while cheering everyone on. I came again, but still I wanted more. What was in the wine? I wanted more, yet each time was pleasurable. The red headed woman walked up and sticking out of her robe was a dildo the size of cucumber. She grinned and I opened my robe letting her in. She pushed it into me and we fell onto a nearby couch. It was a double ended dildo pleasuring us both. It didn't take long for us to come in a shuttering climax.

The black pixie was on her knees with her head under a man's robe. It was all so polite with everyone robed. No tits showed. Hardly any skin. A robe would be parted to allow someone or something to reach in or for something to stick out for someone to pounce on.

I was fucked about seventeen times that night, by both men and women. I was sore and aching but still I wanted more. I gave as much as I received. At one point in the ceremony, a man gently laid me down on a pile of pillows, straddled me and stuck his penis into me. While he was bouncing on me, the red head sat on my face and guided my tongue to her wet singing nub.

The short haired girl took my hand and inserted it into her warm wet pussy and rode up and down on it. Feeling and being felt, fucking and being fucked, I was one large sexual nerve ending. Fuck, fuck, fuck, it was all about fucking and that was it. That was what the world was all about. Just fucking.

I took a taxi home. I could barely walk. The taxi driver helped me in and somehow ended up in my bed. It was so gratifying that men enjoyed me as much as I enjoyed them.

That night was a haze. After the taxi driver left, I lay on top of the covers and was almost asleep when another man in a cab driver's cap stood beside my bed. His penis was bobbing up and down.

"Come on in," I said and I spread my weary legs wide.

"Thank you, ma'am." He tipped his hat which he kept on.

"You're welcome."

He left and the door opened again. This one wore a yellow cap. He lowered his pants and climbed on top of me. He squeezed my breasts as he rode up and down on me. "Oh god, oh god, oh god," he kept saying.

I observed these shenanigans from afar. My consciousness was on the ceiling looking down at the stream of men, coming into my bedroom and dropping their pants or some just unzipping. Penises of all sizes, large, small, fat, and thin came and went and came again. Finally, it was dawn. Somehow I made it to the door and locked it. When the buzzer sounded I ignored it.

27: The Super-Fast Super

I slept all day and all the next night and when I woke up I phoned the super and said I would take the penthouse apartment he had kindly let me know was coming up. To thank him for the favour, I promised him one. We both knew what that favour would be.

I phoned work and said I was unavailable for the week. I never wanted to see a penis for at least that long.

The super pestered me when he could collect his favour. I told him the day I moved in.

Two weeks passed, and I stayed off work and stayed away from men. It was as if I'd been fucked out of all desire or some such strange thing. It didn't bother me either. My body needed a rest.

The next week, the movers came and moved me upstairs. Neither of them made a pass at me or I, them. That didn't hit me until they'd left.

What the hell had happened to me? Virginia had started to stir a little so that was a good sign.

It was an easy move, and all the furniture was set in the right places. I had a few boxes around and started to dig in when the door chime went.

It was the Super with his hand on his fly and a gleam in his eye. My fully blown desire for sex hadn't returned yet but maybe this would give it a start.

He grabbed me where I stood, pulled my track pants and under pants down and just before he plunged it in, I said, "This is a one time deal. Agreed?"

He groaned yes very quickly, and did his business very quickly. He was in and out and finished before I had barely started. I stood there stunned. Virginia too wondered what the blur had been.

He zipped up. "Thank you ma'm. That was mighty fine. Are you available next week, same time?"

I pulled up my pants. "Absolutely not. This was a one off."

He looked downfallen. "But I heard you liked to be fucked."

"Where the hell did you hear that?"

"I saw you had a lot of policemen visitors a while back and I couldn't help but notice you needed a lot of taxi's a few weeks ago."

It was my time to groan. "How observant of you."

"Once you get used to me, you'll love it. There's a lady in 126 and another in 301 that I see once a week."

"That's nice for you, but this is one lady you won't be seeing again, unless it's for a drippy tap or some other household calamity."

"I'm available anytime. If you change your mind, give me a call."

"I won't change my mind. Goodbye." I shut the door and got to my unpacking.

Next Saturday, there was a ring at my door. He stood there, his hand on the top of his zipper. "Are you ready for some fun?"

I couldn't believe this man. He thought his performance was fun? "No, thank you." I started to close the door and he put his foot in the way.

"I'll be quick."

I'm sure he would be but that wasn't the point. Virginia twitched a little, but I still wasn't into sex yet. I was still waiting for the urge and he certainly hadn't stimulated it.

"Pretty please with sugar on it." He stepped in and closed the door behind him.

Virginia throbbed a little more. *I guess I could try one more time. Maybe it will stir up my sex drive.* "Oh, alright. Just one more time."

The glee in his eyes overflowed. He pulled up my skirt, pulled down my pants and there was his big pecker pushing into me. God, that man was fast. In and out and bang. Finished.

"Thank you ma'm. That was grand." He zipped up. "Did you like that?"

"Liked what?"

He laughed. "My other ladies say I'm a little fast. Just can't help it. But you'll get used to it."

And he was gone. "I don't think so," I called after him.

I couldn't believe it. In two days, he was at the door again, his hand on his zipper. I had started to have a little urge for some good sex but not this way.

"You're just too fast for me," I said. "I'm not just some receptacle you dump into. Sex should be a mutual pleasure."

"But I want to pleasure you. I just can't help it. My pecker has a mind of its own."

"Maybe if you think of something else, it will slow things down."

"But I can't think of anything else. I go on the internet every minute I can and look at nude ladies and masturbate. Then when I'm with a real live lady, I think of those bare naked ones and—bang."

"That's your problem. Think of something else when you're with a lady. Think of leaky taps or broken pipes."

He hung his head. "I could try."

Oh, dear. I started to feel sorry for him. Maybe I could help him learn how to pleasure his ladies. "Come in. And take our hand off your zipper. We are just going to sit and have a cup of tea."

"But I want—'

"I know what you want and you will get it." This was beginning to feel like a little fun. "We're just going to take our time."

"You mean you'll let me do it to you?"

"No."

His eyes got big.

"I'm not going to let you do it TO me. We are going to do it together. Big difference."

He followed me to the kitchen where I made tea. We sat at the kitchen table and we talked about his work and my work and the weather and even a smattering of politics. Anything but sex.

His buzzer went. He clicked it on. "I have to check out a leak in 638."

"Do you have to go right now?"

"No. It's not an emergency. Why?"

"Well, we've had such a nice visit. Would you like to lie down for a moment?"

His eyes got big and he reached for his zipper.

"No. Take your hand away from there. We are just going to lie beside each other. Fully clothed."

"Really. I've never done anything like that before."

We went into the bedroom and took off our shoes and lay down not touching.

"What do we do now?" he said.

"You could hug me, but that's all."

"Okay." He rolled over and put his arms around me. "Now what?"

"We just lie here for another moment."

We did and then I said, "Do you think you could take your pecker out without having it explode? I just want to look at it, that's all. I won't touch it."

"I—I'll try."

"Think of the work you have to do in Apartment 638."

"Okay."

He slowly slid his zipper down. *Good start.* He pulled out his pecker. *So far so good.* His face got red and he held his breath. "How are you doing?" I said.

"Barely holding on. I can't—"

"Okay, okay. Don't panic. Breath." I lifted my skirt and pulled my pants down. "I'm going to lie on top of you. You just lie there and let me do the work."

He didn't say anything. I think he was still holding his breath as well as his pecker. I rolled on top of him, placing Virginia on the tip of his throbbing penis. Slowly I pushed myself down on him.

He gasped and started pumping like mad. What could a girl do? I let him have his way. I couldn't have stopped him anyway. I was just starting to enjoy it when bang he came and collapsed on top of me.

"Sorry, sorry, I couldn't help it. But that's the longest I've ever lasted. Thank you. Thank you." He pulled out of me and rolled off.

"We're not finished yet? At least I'm not."

"What do you mean?"

"You need to finish me off. Men aren't the only ones in this game to explode. Ladies want their turn as well."

"What do you mean?"

I couldn't believe this man didn't know that ladies had organisms too. I had to teach this man for the sake of his other lady friends. We gals have to stick together. I took his hand. "Put your fingers in me and make me come."

"What?"

"Just do it." I was getting a little frustrated and since I had a man there I wasn't going to finish myself off.

He stuck two fat fingers into me and slid in and out. I wriggled with him making sure he hit my sweet spots. Just when I was about to burst I felt a thick penis fill me, thrusting like a wild horse and both our rockets exploded at the same time.

We lay there for many minutes before he slid out of me.

"Whew," he said. "That was a miracle."

"It was pretty nice, I have to say."

"I never knew that ladies could come like that."

I leaned up on one elbow. "What do you mean? I'm sure you saw some videos of ladies in the throws of delight."

"Oh, sure, but I thought they were all faking. I didn't know they could actually feel anything."

I shook my head. "Now that you know do you think you'll be having more fun with your lady friends, making them as happy as you?'

A big smile. "I'm sure going to try."

We lay there for a few more minutes. He said, "Do you think we could try that again? I want to be sure I can make you happy."

"You mean right now?" I wasn't sure I wanted another fuck so soon.

"Not if you don't want to."

"I'm still enjoying the last one."

"If I need more practice, can I come back?"

He looked like a little boy who had just learned how to throw a ball. "Perhaps," I said.

His buzzer went again, and he left to deal with Apartment 638.

Three days later, he was at my door with a bouquet of flowers.

"What are these for?"

He stepped in."For giving me the best gift ever."

I took them into the kitchen and put them in a vase. "What gift was that?"

"For showing me how to give pleasure to the ladies. Both my lady friends are eternally grateful. And they're teaching me how to make them even happier."

"And is that okay with you?"

"It's more than okay. It's fantastic. I get to fuck two or three times each visit. They never tire and I am slowing down even more to give us both more excitement."

I smiled. It felt nice to do a good deed for a fellow man.

He made a little bow. "If you would like, I would be glad to show how far I'm come."

Virginia nodded yes and my thighs tingled. We went to the bedroom and he every so patiently, undressed me, kissed my boobs several times before the first medium speed fuck. He took off the rest of his clothes and when I'd recovered, he proudly fucked me again, starting slow and building up to a very lovely crescendo of mutual coming. He was indeed a fast learner.

However, my sex drive had changed. I no longer thirsted for a daily fuck and even though a few times with the super reminded me how great sex was, there was something different about it. I wasn't just thinking of dicks, but of the men who had them. Sounds crazy, but men must have feelings too. Maybe there was more to this whole sex stuff.

I needed some time away from men and to think. I booked a two week holiday at a convent in the country.

28: Lessons at the Convent

The taxi drew up to the entrance of the Sisters of The Holy Mother Convent. A sweet faced nun greeted me. Another took my suitcase and another, with hands tucked into her sleeves, nodded for me to follow her. They all had sweet faces. I settled into my cell—a small room with a cot, a side table and a crucifix on the wall. Memories of my priestly experience floated up. The poor man must have wondered what hit him. I hoped I hadn't done him harm. But I don't believe in coincidence so maybe we were destined to meet for both our reasons.

The convent was a very restful place, except for the bells. They rang intermittently all through the day and night, calling meal time, prayer time, and work time for the regular inhabitants. The visitors were free to partake in whatever they needed.

For two days, I slept and ate and on the third took a walk in the cloistered gardens. Another woman was on silent retreat and when we passed she averted her gaze or lowered her head. Like a ghost. That was fine. I needed solitude. Time to think and to just be me, whoever that was.

Was I just a vagina? Had all my sexual activity been to make up for fifty frigid years? If so, I had done a pretty good job of it. I wondered if I would ever want sex again, with man, woman or self administered.

After a week, I was surprised that I wasn't rushing into the nearest town to find a man with a big dick. At least I put man first.

My body felt used and I apologized to it for pushing it to the brink. Perhaps too much sex was too much. I wasn't a machine. I saw a notice on the bulletin board offering Therapeutic Massage. That would be good.

The next day, I lay naked on my stomach under a soft sheet on a high cushioned table. My whole body luxuriated in comfort. A young woman, dressed in a white robe came in.

"Are you a nun," I asked.

"A postulant."

"What's that?"

"I am in training to be a nun. It is a time for me to decide whether to take final vows."

"Oh. And are you a massage therapist?"

"I was for ten years, but my parents wanted me to be a nun."

I thought that was a crazy reason to become a nun, but I didn't say anything.

She lowered the sheet to my waist and I felt a gentle hand on my back along with the smell of lavender. "That feels so good," I said.

"Just relax and let go."

It was nice to be touched asexually. Under her gentle hands, my body rested and slowly gathered itself back together as one entity. I was not just a vagina, a cunt, a hole to be filled. Or two soft breasts to be fondled, and sucked and licked like they were not part of me. These parts were parts of a whole me.

The next day I had another massage by the same young woman. Virginia tingled as she touched me. But it was a different tingle. Not just at that spot. My whole body shivered, wanting to be stroked and loved, and I wanted to be kissed.

In my whole crazy year of fuckdom, I never wanted the men to kiss me and they never did. I only wanted a fuck and a quick goodbye. Tom was the only one who had. He had awakened me with a kiss. A kiss that started the whole adventure between my legs.

On my third massage, when I turned over and was lying on my back, she had placed a towel over my breasts while she massaged my stomach area. My whole body, my self wanted her to move her hands all over me, to touch me sexually. To make physical love to me.

I pushed the feeling away, but the impulse was so strong. Next I heard myself saying, "Would you like to touch my breasts?" I slid the towel off completely.

She flushed. "I'm sorry."

"Since you're still a postulate, would it break any rules?" *What am I saying? Leave the girl alone.* But I continued. "You're touch has been so healing to me. It doesn't feel wrong if you would touch me other places. In fact my body yearns for it."

Her hands and voice shook. "I was thinking I wanted to. You must have read my mind."

"We are two consenting adults. It would be all right." My whole self was crying to be caressed by this gentle soul.

Her lovely soft hands, moist from lavender oil, cupped a breast and she leaned over and she put her mouth on my nipple. Her angel tongue licked and she sucked ever so gently. From one to the other she moved like a ballet dancer. Music seemed to fill the air and I was floating. I held her head covered with the cloth of a nun and wondered what her hair felt like.

My hips started moving on their own, up and down. Virginia ached to be part of this wonderful woman's touch and before I knew it was guiding her head and hands lower and lower.

She didn't resist, kissing my stomach, and down to my bush and to my wet and ready opening. Her tongue easily found its way to electrifying spots and I pushed against her in uncontrolled spasms. She pulled my buttocks up to get deeper inside me and I revelled in such pleasure as my soul and body every knew.

Who was the teacher here? Not I. I came in an ecstasy of delight and afterward lay like a new born baby welcomed into life.

She took a towel and mopped me and her face. "I'm so sorry. I don't know what came over me."

I smiled up at her from the depths of fulfillment. "Whatever it was, it was God sent. Are you sure you want to be a nun?"

She lowered her head. "What we did was a sin in God's eyes. I have been beaten for it."

I took her hand. "My dear. What we did is not a sin in God's eyes. Only in misinformed, ignorant and prejudiced human eyes."

She glanced up. "My parents thought otherwise. That's why they sent me here. To correct my evil ways."

"Who you are is perfectly natural. Don't be embarrassed, or ashamed. It is not wrong to love a woman."

She hung her head.

I reached for her hand and she let me take it."What's your name?" I asked.

"Rebecca."

"That's a lovely name. I looked around the small room. Are we private here?"

"Yes, but the door is not locked."

"Lock it."

She looked at me for a long moment and went to the door and locked it.

"It's your turn." I said. "You lie on the table."

Her eyes opened wide. "I couldn't. My robes—"

"Take them off.

She plastered both hands on her chest. "I couldn't. I only take them off at bedtime and never in front of anyone, especially another woman."

I walked over to her, took her face in my hands and put my mouth on hers. Such soft and yielding lips. Our tongues searched each other, gently and then more urgently—one naked woman and one dressed as a postulant deciding if she would be a nun.

It wasn't long before we were both naked and lying on a soft rug on the floor. Limbs entwined, pushing against each other. Our fingers and tongues seeking and finding wet welcome entrances, bringing us to the brink again and again until total surrender to the mystery and ecstasy of complete and utter coupling. We were one. I didn't know where I ended and she began. We were one body of light in God's presence and She smiled upon us.

I stayed at the convent for another week. Every night I would make my way to her room or she to mine. Some nights we just talked but most of the time we would make love. I'd never called sex making love before, but this felt like it.

One evening, sitting side by side, we were well into it—our fingers moving in and out of each other, and kissing like there was no tomorrow when the door opened. A shaft of light stretched across us and we jumped apart.

A voice came around the door. "Rebecca? Is someone with you?"

It was postulate Marguerite from across the hall.

"I thought I heard heavy breathing and I wondered if you were all right."

"I am quite fine, Marguerite. Come in."

She walked in and stopped. We were of course both naked.

"Oh, my. What is happening here?"

We both laughed and I said, "We are making beautiful love."

"Oh, my. Are we allowed to pleasure ourselves that way?

Rebecca said. "It's the most natural thing in the world. Why not?"

"But how can you do it with women? They don't have —you know. The equipment."

We both laughed again. "Oh, my dear," I said. " A penis is very nice if you want one, but you don't need one.

Fingers, tongues, even toes are great substitutes." I paused. "Have you ever tried it with a woman?"

She just stood there but she didn't run away.

Rebecca lifted her hand to her. "Oh, do come and join us, dear sister. You may find you'll like it."

She was hesitant at first but we ended up having a very satisfying evening of teaching and learning the many ways of pleasuring each other.

A week later, it was time for me to go. Rebecca had done some deep thinking and since it was never her idea to be a nun, in fact it was punishment from her parents, she decided she would not take her final vows. She would proudly and with face lifted, be who she was born to be—a woman who loves a woman. She would return to her first and only love who had been sent away as well. She would find her and I promised her I would help if she needed any.

"Thank you," she said. "You have given me my life back by opening my mind to the truth. Each person must follow their own guidance and find their way back to their destiny, even if it means rejecting parental and the church's human-made rules. Stupid, ignorant rules that are not the heart's truth."

I kissed her and Marguerite goodbye and climbed into the taxis to take me back to the city. To what?

As I waved goodbye the question hung heavy within me. Who was I? I had been a frigid, uptight woman who tolerated her husband's Saturday night gyrations. Then I was a wild sex addict lusting for a hot dick, and now a lesbian—or at least a woman with a wonderful lesbian experience. What about men? I had to know if I could still enjoy sex with a man.

Several times, as the taxi drove through the countryside on its way back to my waiting apartment I looked in the driver's mirror and caught him looking at me. He was a young good looking guy and I certainly knew that men at that age were ready all the time. Come to think of it, not just that age. He would be a good test to see if I had gone off men.

We were still in the country side and I suggested we stop to admire that soft spot of grass by that winding river.

He didn't mind stopping. He was a musician and was only driving taxis until his next gig. So we climbed over the split rail fence, walked down a little incline to the river side and sat on the grass.

I lay back and looked up at the trees. He lay beside me and asked if I was comfortable. I nodded yes, and he put his hand on my breast. When I didn't object he undid my blouse and my bra and put his face where is hand had been.

He didn't rush and it was nice to handled so gently. He seemed to like being with an older woman and after some very nice fondling and licking my breasts he pulled my skirt up. I was pleased that Virginia was eagerly wet and impatiently waiting, and when he did put his penis deep inside me, that old familiar feeling of being at home, being with the highest and best I could be, filled me.

We fucked our way through the Milky Way and beyond and I thanked all the Gods and Goddesses for making me a woman.

Epilogue

I settled back in the taxi fully assured I still liked sex with men. I guessed that I was now bi-sexual which was great. I would have the whole population to choose from.

After a few weeks at home and getting settled into my new apartment I was surprised that I hadn't craved sex at all—with man or woman. I did feel restless however, and resigned from my temp job. After thirty years with Industrial, I was getting a decent pension, and Harold had left me financially comfortable.

The super dropped in to welcome me back and apologized he wouldn't be available for sex with me. He had just too many lady friends in the building that he had to attend to.

I told him, no problem and I was glad for his success. I was getting a little concerned, however, that I was not ravenous to indulge in anonymous sex and wondered why I didn't think that the whole point of life was to have a penis in me.

I had done well in school and decided to enrol in the local college in the psychology class. That was an eye opener and I loved the classes. My first year professor was a fascinating man and I enjoyed learning so much. No we didn't indulge in sex, but did indulge in the most enlightening discussions.

In my second year, he wasn't my professor and he asked me out on a date. A date! It had been years since I had been on a real date. Well, I guess when Tom took me to the bar after my birthday awakening had been a date, but this was different.

I was also astounded that I hadn't had sex for over a year. What astounded me more was that I didn't even miss it. I got buried in my studies and it was enough.

Well, not quite. My ex-professor and I went out several more times and to my utter surprise we fell in love. Ironically his name was Tom too. It seems that Tom's are life changers for me.

The next year I received my counsellors certificate and Tom and I got married. Yes, can you believe it. I had actually fallen in love. The first time we had sex was another awakening. In fact, we didn't *have sex*, we made love. The sex seemed to just be a natural part of what we wanted to express to each other. I never knew it could be like that.

We moved into the penthouse of the harbour front apartments. The first two floors were offices and I set up my practise in one of them as fully fledged, licensed sex therapist.

They say the best therapist are the ones who have been through it, well, as you know I certainly had.

So that is the story of my adventures of being a sex addict and through that learned what sex really is. Yes, it can take you to the moon and back, but ladies and gentleman I implore you to search deep within yourself and do the best for you. Love yourself first. Get rid of the hob goblins and false truths you were brought up with.

There is and never has been anything wrong with you. You are loved by the greatest force in the Universe.

Everyone you meet, and every experience you have is for you to discover more about yourself. And when you discover that you are not only made of love, but are love you will not feel driven or scared or lost or ashamed or guilty or afraid or abandoned or alone ever again.

You will discover you are enough, in fact more than enough. You are a worthwhile and much loved person.

My best wishes go with you on your journey.

* * *

And please, if you would, I would really appreciate it if you would leave a review on Amazon to let other browers and book lovers know how much you enjoyed reading this book.

Thank you.

Sherry Marie Somerville..

www.ingramcontent.com/pod-product-compliance
Lightning Source LLC
Chambersburg PA
CBHW060426130626
46555CB00005B/2230